SECRETS OF THE FORSAKEN

Selected Books by the Editors

Embrace Your Divine Flow:
Evolvements for Healing

Julian Hobson and Lorene Shyba, Eds.

The Art of Making:
Rediscovering the Blackfoot Legacy

Jared Tailfeathers

Indigenous Justice:
True Cases by Judges, Lawyers, and
Law Enforcement Officers

Lorene Shyba and Raymond Yakeleya, Eds.

SECRETS OF THE FORSAKEN

JULIAN HOBSON
LORENE SHYBA
JARED TAILFEATHERS

EDS.

DURVILE & UpRoute
DURVILE.COM

Calgary, Alberta, Canada

DURVILE.COM

DURVILE & UpRoute

UpRoute Imprint of Durvile Publications Ltd.
Calgary, Alberta, Canada
www.durvile.com

Library and Archives Cataloging in Publication Data

SECRETS OF THE FORSAKEN: INTO THE DEPTHS OF DREAD
Julian Hobson; Lorene Shyba; Jared Tailfeathers;
Cary Thomas Cody; Jessica Theroux; Raymond Yakeleya; Maeve Wills;
Alex Soop; Laurier Tiernan; Lynda Partridge; Uchechukwu Umezurike;
John L. Hill; James R. Parker; Mary Shelley; Virginia Woolf;
Ryūnosuke Akutagawa; Helena Blavatsky; Mark Twain; Ambrose Bierce

1. Horror | 2. Paranormal | 3. Indigenous | 4. Supernatural | 5. Romantasy

The UpRoute "Spirit of Nature" Series
A "Ways of Light and Darkness" Title

Issued in print and electronic formats
ISBN: 978-1-990735-90-5 (pbk); 978-1-990735-91-2 (e-pub);
978-1-990735-81-3 (audiobook)

Front cover and illustrations by Julian Hobson. Book design by Lorene Shyba.
Artwork was created using traditional pen and ink techniques,
digital editing, and AI-assisted prompt art.

Durvile Publications greatly acknowledges financial support for
book development and production from the
Government of Canada through Canadian Heritage, Canada Book Fund
and the Government of Alberta, Alberta Media Fund.

Canada Alberta Government

We acknowledge the Traditional Landa of the Treaty 7 Peoples of Southern Alberta,
including the Siksika, Piikani, and Kainai of the Blackfoot Confederacy;
the Dene Tsuut'ina; and the Goodstoney, Chiniki, and Bearspaw Stoney Nakoda First Nations.
We also honour the Homeland of the Otipemisiwak Métis Nation of Alberta.

Printed and bound in Canada. First Printing, 2025.

To the Lost …

The Light

Will

Find

You

CONTENTS

CONTENTS

PART ONE

SECRETS UNEARTHED

Original Writings from Living Authors

"I am Lucifer," his voice
tinged with an ancient sorrow.
"The Morning Star,
the first of all to rise."

1

THE KNOCK OF DAMNATION

Julian Hobson

IN THE YEAR of our Lord 1850, the town of Ashwood lay nestled in a valley often shrouded in a mist so thick, it seemed as if the heavens themselves wished to conceal it from the world. Ashwood was not unlike any other sleepy English village, save for one peculiar tradition—the knocker-uppers. These early risers, equipped with long poles and a keen sense of duty, went from house to house, tapping on windows and rousing the villagers from their slumber.

Among them was a man by the name of Thomas Wychwood. Thomas was diligent, never once shirking his responsibility. He was a man of average stature and modest means, but in his heart, there was a weight that grew with each passing day. Married to Margaret, a gentle woman of quiet grace, and father to two sprightly children, Mary and John, Thomas should have been content. Yet, as the years passed, he felt as though a shadow hovered over him, growing darker with each passing dawn.

Every morning, without fail, Thomas awoke and began his rounds. The tapping of his stick on the glass became a part of the town's rhythm, a beat that synchronized with the daily grind of life. But there was something peculiar about Thomas's own mornings—something that gnawed at the back of his mind. He could not recall ever waking of his own accord. Each day began in a haze, his limbs moving as if compelled by a force he could not name. His nights, too, were plagued by dreams of fire and shadow, though the details were always lost upon waking.

One foggy evening, as the moon hung low and pale over Ashwood, Thomas completed his rounds and found himself standing at the edge of town. The air had grown unnaturally cold, and the silence was so profound that even the nocturnal creatures dared not stir. It was then that Thomas noticed a figure standing beneath the twisted branches of a great oak tree, cloaked in shadows so deep they seemed to swallow the light.

"Who wakes the knocker-upper?" the figure asked, his voice like the crackling of embers in a dying fire.

Thomas's heart seized in his chest, his mouth dry as dust. The figure stepped forward, and though his features remained shrouded, the power of his presence was undeniable.

"I am Lucifer," the figure continued, his voice tinged with an ancient sorrow. "The Morning Star, the first of all to rise."

At the utterance of that dread name, Thomas felt a chill that penetrated to his very soul. Lucifer—the fallen angel, cast from the grace of Heaven into the abyss. The name was whispered in every sermon, a warning to all who might stray from the path of righteousness. Yet here he stood before Thomas, not as a terrible demon, but as something infinitely more tragic.

"I have walked this earth long, Thomas Wychwood," Lucifer said, his voice low and mournful. "I was once the brightest of all angels, beloved of God. But in my pride, I sought to challenge Him, to be His equal. For that, I was cast down, and I have roamed the shadows ever since."

Lucifer's eyes, glowing faintly like distant stars, fixed on Thomas with a gaze that seemed to pierce the very fabric of his being. "You are my servant, bound to me by an infernal chain you cannot see. Each morning, you rise because I will it. You wake the townspeople not merely from sleep, but into a life of toil and misery. You are the knocker of damnation, and with each tap of your stick, you bind the souls of Ashwood to the same drudgery that binds you."

Thomas staggered back, his mind reeling. Could it be true? All these years, he had thought himself a humble man, performing a simple task for the good of the town. But now, confronted by this dark truth, he felt the ground shift beneath him. He was not just a knocker-upper; he was a harbinger of suffering, perpetuating a cycle of despair.

But Lucifer, despite his power, did not gloat. Instead, there was a deep sorrow in his voice, a sorrow that stretched back to the dawn of time.

"I am not here to gloat, Thomas," Lucifer said, as if reading his thoughts. "I am here because I, too, am bound. My rebellion, my fall—it was born of pride, of a desire to control. But what I did not understand, what I could not see, was that in seeking to rule, I severed myself from the very thing that gave my existence meaning—God's love."

At this, Lucifer's voice broke, and for a moment, the air was thick with the weight of his grief. "I have been lost in the darkness for millennia, a prisoner of my own making. And yet, even now, I feel the pull of that love, distant though it may be. For God, in His infinite mercy, has never forsaken me. His forgiveness has always been there, waiting for me to reach out and take it."

Thomas stared at Lucifer in disbelief. Could it be true? Could God forgive even the greatest of sinners, the one who had defied Him and been cast into the pit of despair? And if so, what did that mean for Thomas, who had unwittingly served this dark master?

As if in answer to his unspoken question, a presence filled the air—a presence so vast and so compassionate that it seemed to transcend the very fabric of reality. It was not a voice that spoke, but a feeling—a warmth, a light, a love so profound that it enveloped Thomas and Lucifer alike.

"Lucifer," came the silent communication, "My forgiveness has always been yours to take. I cast you down, not out of wrath, but because you could not remain in Heaven while you rejected love. But love, My love, is eternal, and it has never left you."

Lucifer bowed his head, tears slipping from his eyes, and for the first time in eons, he spoke not as the Morning Star, but as a soul seeking redemption. "Father," he whispered, "I was blind, lost in my own pride. I see now the folly of my rebellion, the emptiness of the power I sought. But I do not know if I am worthy of Your forgiveness."

"Forgiveness is not earned, my son," the presence communicated. "It is given freely to all who seek it. But your journey is not yet complete. You must continue to walk in the shadows, not as their ruler, but as an observer. You will walk with Thomas and witness the love that flows from the hearts of those you once sought to control. And in time, you will understand the true power of love."

Lucifer nodded, his head still bowed, his once-proud wings now folded in submission.

Thomas, overwhelmed by the enormity of what was unfolding before him, felt a sudden clarity. He had spent his life in fear—fear of the unknown, fear of failure, fear of death. But now, as the divine presence washed over him, all that fear melted away, replaced by a profound understanding.

In that moment, Thomas saw the universe as it truly was—a vast, interconnected web of light and darkness, good and evil, love and fear. He saw that the darkness existed not as an equal force to the light, but as a shadow cast by it. The darkness, in its pride, believed itself to be powerful, but it existed only because the light allowed it to. And the light—God's love—was the true force that held all things together.

Thomas realized that his purpose was not to serve the darkness, but to bring light into the shadows. He was not merely a knocker-upper; he was a messenger of love, a beacon of hope in a world often consumed by despair.

And Lucifer, the fallen Morning Star, would walk beside him, learning the lessons of love and forgiveness that he had once rejected.

As Thomas looked out over the town of Ashwood, he no longer saw a place of toil and misery. He saw a community, bound together by love, even in their darkest moments. He saw the faces of his wife and children, and he understood, with a clarity that brought tears to his eyes, that love was the force that would save them all.

Lucifer stood beside him, his once fiery eyes now softened with understanding. "The darkness will always exist," Lucifer said quietly, "but it no longer holds the power it once did. It cannot, for now I see that it is the light that gives it form. And perhaps, one day, I will return to that light. Perhaps."

Thomas nodded. He had no fear of the future, no fear of the unknown. He had seen the truth of the universe, and it was love.

And so, the tale of Ashwood continued, but with a new rhythm. Thomas Wychwood, the knocker-upper, no longer tapped the windows with dread, but with a quiet joy. For with each knock, he was not waking the damned, but reminding them of the light that shone within them. And as for Lucifer, the Morning Star, he walked beside Thomas, no longer a prince of darkness, but a soul in search of redemption.

In time, the balance of light and dark would shift again, as it always does. But Thomas knew, deep in his heart, that the light would always prevail, for the darkness could never exist without it. And in that knowledge, there was peace.

"She couldn't shake the feeling that he was being dragged into something very dangerous."

2

THE BEACH

Lorene Shyba

LARA SAT ON THE DAMP SAND, watching the last light slip below the horizon. It was quiet except for the waves rolling in, steady and unhurried. Tonight was supposed to be different. Antony needed the break; she knew it, and so did he. His music was good—better than good. But nobody noticed, and he carried that around like a stone in his pocket, always weighing him down. They'd planned to keep it simple. Dinner, a walk on the beach, maybe time to work on that new song. But now she was sitting there alone, and the sand was cold.

Antony had been pulled away by a single phone call.

The moment she heard Anne's voice on the other end, Lara felt it—a cold, familiar tension. Anne's voice always had that sharp, insistent edge when she spoke to Antony, like she needed something only he could give. Lara wasn't part of these family conversations, and tonight was no different. Antony shifted nervously, unable to meet her gaze.

"I've got to go. It's ... Anne," he muttered, eyes flicking from his phone to the ground.

"Now?" Lara asked, a knot tightening in her chest.

"I'll make it up to you," he said, fumbling for his wallet. He handed her a crumpled twenty, like it could somehow smooth over the moment. "Just get yourself dinner, okay?"

Lara stared at the bill, not reaching for it. "I don't want your money. I wanted to be with you."

But Antony didn't linger. He walked away, his figure fading into the distance, leaving her behind with only the growing dark and the sound of the waves. The sun had slipped below the horizon and the shadows crept in, long and eerie, swallowing the beach whole. Lara's mind raced with questions. What could be so important that Antony would forsake her like this? And why did Anne always seem to pull him into things without her?

She felt sick. She had never liked Antony's sister Anne—her icy demeanor, the condescending way she spoke, always reminding Lara that she didn't belong. And now, there was something darker at play. Lara couldn't shake the feeling that Antony was being dragged into something dangerous, something beyond a family issue. With a frustrated sigh, Lara pushed herself up from the sand and dusted off her skirt. She couldn't sit there feeling abandoned. She needed to know what was happening. She needed to find Antony.

The walk to Anne and Mike's beach house wasn't far, but each step felt heavier than the last. As Lara drew closer, the sight of the house stopped her in her tracks. The quaint beach cottage now looked more like a haunted relic; its edges blurred in the growing twilight. The windows, usually open to the breeze, were tightly shuttered, and a faint, flickering light glowed from behind drawn shades. No other light came from within, making the house appear like a slumbering beast, waiting. A shiver ran down Lara's spine.

She stood there for a moment, taking it all in. The house pulsed with an energy that didn't belong. The salty air that normally felt refreshing now felt thick, as though the house itself was breathing in the darkness around it. The longer she stared, the more ominous it became, as if warning her to turn back. But she couldn't. Antony was inside.

With a deep breath, Lara forced herself to continue. She hesitated only for a moment, her hand trembling as it turned the doorknob. The air within was stifling, thick with the scent of burning wax and something else—something metallic, like the sharp tang of blood. Candles lined every surface, their dim glow casting long, distorted shadows that danced across the walls. The room was bathed in an eerie, flickering glow, making everything appear as though it was swaying in time with the shadows.

Lara's heart pounded in her chest as the realization hit

This was a séance.

In the centre of the room, a circle of people sat—Anne, Mike, and three strangers. The strangers looked sharp, their faces obscured by the half-light, but they exuded a sense of power and danger. There was something undeniably sinister about them. Their clothes were too crisp, their movements too precise. Lara couldn't shake the feeling that they had shed their normal lives the moment they entered this room.

But it was the figure in the middle of the circle that truly stole Lara's breath. The fortune teller sat on a low stool, her posture unnervingly still. She was draped in heavy, dark robes that absorbed the light, making her appear like a shadow come to life. Layers of black and deep-purple fabric cascaded around her, hiding her feet, and long, fingerless gloves clung to her forearms, revealing her gnarled, bony fingers. Her face was hidden beneath a hood, but from the faint flicker of candlelight, Lara caught glimpses of pale skin, wrinkled and stretched, like parchment over bone.

Her hands, raised slightly in the air, moved in slow, deliberate circles. Each movement was hypnotic, as though she was weaving something unseen into the very air around her. Every so often, her fingers twitched, and the shadows in the room flickered in response. Lips murmuring inaudible words. Around her neck hung a necklace of strange, mismatched trinkets—bones, feathers, and stones that glimmered in the candlelight. Her presence dominated the room, a gravitational force that held everyone in its orbit. She was watching as power was being summoned, twisted, and manipulated by a force far older than anyone in that room understood.

"Antony!" Lara's voice came out louder than she'd intended. The entire room froze, heads snapping toward her in unison. Antony was standing awkwardly near the edge of the group, looking as though he wished he could sink into the floor.

"Lara, what are you doing here?" His voice wavered, panic flashing in his eyes.

Anne stood abruptly, her face twisted with anger. "You weren't invited." Her voice was sharp, venomous, cutting through the thick air. "This isn't for you."

"I just want to know what's going on," Lara said, stepping further into the room despite the suffocating tension.

"This is business," Anne spat. "Something you wouldn't understand."

"She doesn't belong here," one of the strangers growled, his eyes narrowing at Lara.

Lara's eyes darted to Antony, silently pleading for him to say something, anything. But he just stood there, looking apologetic, uselessly blowing her a kiss from across the room as if that would make up for everything.

"You should've stayed on the beach," he mumbled.

Tears stung Lara's eyes as humiliation washed over her. Without another word, she turned and fled back to the beach. By the time she reached the shore again, the sun had fully set, leaving the world in darkness. She felt sick, her heart pounding in her chest. What had she walked in on? What were they doing?

The waves shimmered in the faint light of the moon, their gentle motion the only comfort she had left. But then something changed. The shimmering grew brighter, more intense, and from the water, something began to emerge. Lara gasped as a figure slithered from the depths—a grotesque, twisted form of luminous water and fire, its shape shifting and pulsing as it moved. It gleamed with an unholy light. When it spoke, its voice was a chorus of hissing whispers.

"They think they summon power," it rasped, "but they summon me."

Lara took a step back, her breath catching in her throat. "What are you?"

The terrifying presence smiled, a horrifying, twisted grin. "I am the lie they desire."

With a flash of fire, the entity vanished, leaving Lara standing alone on the dark beach, her mind reeling. Whatever that thing was, it was heading for the séance—and it wasn't going to bring them fortune. It was going to bring them ruin.

Inside the house, the séance had resumed, but the air had become thick with an unsettling tension. Suddenly, with a deafening knock and a howling gust of wind, a violent surge of energy erupted into the room, sending objects flying from shelves and rattling the walls. Candles flickered wildly, their flames struggling. The poltergeist became visible, slithering across the floor as a grotesque mass of writhing ectoplasm, glowing with a sickly, luminous light. Tendrils of the ectoplasm stretched out like searching fingers, twisting and coiling in the flickering candlelight, as if it was both formless and painfully alive. The air crackled as it rose up, a sinister veil of mist and fire, declaring its dominance over the terrified room.

The medium's eyes widened in horror. Her hands, once steady and weaving magic, trembled uncontrollably. Without warning, she staggered to her feet, tripping over her robes as she scrambled to gather her things. Her eyes darted frantically, panic seizing her as the ectoplasmic mass crept closer. A freezing gust tore through the room, extinguishing the candles with a sharp hiss. Shadows twisted as the temperature dropped. The medium let out a strangled scream, a sound of pure terror, and bolted for the door, yanking it open. She fled into the night, but as she did, the door slammed shut behind her, sealing the others inside with the poltergeist.

"I am the boss now," the entity growled, its voice a deep, guttural rumble that reverberated through the very walls. The room shook with the weight of its presence, and the others sat frozen, eyes wide in terror, unable to move or even breathe. "You've summoned me for fortune, for power," it hissed, the words dripping with mockery, "and I will tell you exactly what you want to hear." As it moved closer, its veil-like tendrils began to unfurl, slow and deliberate, winding around their arms and legs, locking them in place.

One of the strangers, a woman, was paralyzed with fear. As a prominent defence lawyer, she was known for her silver tongue that wove lies so skillfully that her clients in the criminal underworld often escaped justice. The poltergeist sensed this, focusing on her first. "You," it rasped, eyes glowing as it looked into her soul. "Your future is filled with wealth and fame. A golden career, built on the backs of lies. You will become a television star, showcasing your talents for the world to see." The lawyer blinked, her fear melting into smug satisfaction. But outside, on the beach, Lara saw something different. The shimmering waves flickered, revealing a truth the others couldn't see. In the glistening water, Lara saw the lawyer in prison, trapped in a cell, her face twisted with regret as the weight of her crimes finally caught up to her.

The entity turned to the next stranger, a doctor who treated bullet wounds and patched up criminals when they needed to disappear from public hospitals. "You," its voice softer now. "You will possess the power of life itself. Your hands will heal instantly. Wounds will close at your touch. No one will die under your care." The doctor grinned, visibly relieved, but again, the waves outside told another story. Lara watched in horror as the shimmering ocean revealed the truth—this doctor would die of an overdose, alone in a filthy alley, a victim of the very addiction he had ignored in his patients.

Next came the police officer, the one who turned a blind eye to the black market dealings, allowing Anne and Mike's network to operate freely. "For you," the entity whispered, circling her now. "A future of medals and glory. You will rise through the ranks, celebrated for your bravery, untouchable." The police officer nodded, her shoulders relaxing. But the waves outside told a darker tale. Lara saw her gunned down at the scene of a botched robbery, her body lying lifeless in a pool of blood, abandoned by the very criminals she had protected.

The poltergeist then turned to Mike, the restaurateur who moved contraband out the back of his kitchen. "Your empire will grow," the entity promised. "A chain of restaurants from coast to coast. You will be known as the king of cuisine, respected and feared." Mike's eyes gleamed with greed, but again, Lara saw the truth in the waves. He would die from food poisoning in one of his own establishments, a king brought low by his own corruption.

Finally, the creature's gaze landed on Anne. "You, the mastermind," it said almost reverently, feeding off her emotional state. "You will live in a mansion, surrounded by luxury, your real estate empire expanding until there's no one left to challenge you. The world will be yours." Anne's eyes filled with pride, but outside, the shimmering waves showed Lara something else. Anne would end up destitute, betrayed by her own allies, her empire crumbling beneath the weight of her greed. She would die alone, in a dilapidated house, despised and forgotten.

As the poltergeist moved toward Antony, something shifted in the air. It paused, looming over him, but Antony stepped back, shaking his head.

"No," he muttered, his voice trembling. "I don't want this."

The being growled, its form swirling with rage. "You don't get to choose," it snarled. "You summoned me. You seek power like the rest." But Antony shook his head more firmly this time. "No. This isn't me. I'm not like them." He bolted for the door, desperate to escape.

Outside, Lara stood by the waves. When she saw Antony running toward her, she rushed to meet him, her breath catching as he fell into her arms, shaking with fear and regret.

"Lara, I'm sorry," he gasped. "I didn't want any of this. Anne doesn't understand—I just want to make music. Not power. Not money." Lara looked at him, seeing the vulnerability in his eyes. He wasn't made for the life Anne was dragging him into, and she knew it. "Then leave it behind," she whispered.

For a moment, they stood in silence, feeling the weight of their choice settle over them. The beach felt different: calmer, the waves gentle against the shore. The tension that had weighed on them for weeks faded, leaving only the sound of the ocean and the steady beat of their hearts. In the cool night air, Antony felt warmth return, lifting his frustrations and the need to prove himself. It wasn't about fame—it never was. It was the music itself, and Lara was the one who helped him see that. They stood quietly for a long moment, hand in hand, the darkness of Anne's world far behind. Together, they turned and walked down the moonlit beach, his new song quietly taking shape between them.

Inside the house, the tendrils drew back, hissing as they slipped into the poltergeist's core. The glow faded, and the ectoplasm left a slick residue on the walls and floor before vanishing with a final, ominous whisper. The room fell silent. Anne let out a shaky laugh, quickly echoed by the others. They thought it was over. But where the entity had touched, a faint glow lingered—unseen yet clinging to them. The power they had summoned was already tainted; the curse silently marking them for a dark, unavoidable fate.

Be careful. Your friend and his woman. They don't respect it out here. You shouldn't trust them.

3

THE RISING WOLF

Jared Tailfeathers

"I THINK I lost them. I think I lost him... I need to find the trail." He was alone now, out of breath. His feet ached. He was soaking wet. He had to slog through the knee-deep water, freezing cold. The snow had stopped for a minute, releasing the mountains from their white doom. The highest peak stared down at him. A couple of days ago it was beautiful, inviting. Now, it was accusing, a gravestone marking where his friends lay.

Originally, it was going to be a week-long back-camp hike near the Old Man Headwaters. It was late in the camping season. The leaves were almost all gone, there was still just a halo of yellow on a couple of the mountains nearby. In the old ways, you were expected to bring offering. None of the six people who came brought any offering or left it when they went to the cave.

They saw paintings, shield warriors, and figures. They all marvelled at the sight: their history, their people. Even the friends among them who weren't from the Nation felt its weight. They asked questions, cautious yet curious, but they, too, were awestruck by its significance. One of them, however, took something. This was a holy place, a site meant for offerings and gratitude—a space to thank the ancestors for their wisdom. Knowledge is not free.

They camped just outside of that cave, along the water, freezing at night but soaked in beautiful moonlight.

Slim, what a funny name, he laughed to himself. Slim didn't describe him at all. In fact, he was a little bit overweight, but it had stuck with him for his whole life.

Back in his tent, it had been just him. The three other tents had held his friends and their girlfriends—they seemed like nice people. He wished it had been like it had been in the old days, just him and his friends, but they were old now and grown up. Everyone was pressuring him to move on with his life, but he was stuck. People who are stuck don't go anywhere—a living shell, a walking ghost, a spirit that dwells only amidst themselves.

They were six kilometres off the main track. The first two nights had gone without issue, but at some point, early on the third day, something had changed, maybe it had been the night before, around the campfire, telling jokes, singing songs, telling ghost stories. Maggie was a short-time girlfriend of his friend "Soda", the belcher. Maggie had taken something from the cave and had been fiddling around with it in her pocket while we drank around the fire. No one else knew that she had it. They had been warned by family not to take anything from the cave, they were supposed to give something if they wanted to take photos or gain knowledge, but Maggie had taken something, ignorantly, and she fiddled with it. As they sat under the moon and starlight and she began whistling a song, all of his friends stopped. Soda dropped his beer and put his hand over her mouth,

"Shh, we don't whistle at night, what are you doing? I've told you this before."

She hadn't been paying attention though, she never paid attention to any of the cultural stuff, she just thought Soda was handsome.

She responded annoyingly. “Oh, get over it. It’s just a meaningless song. Your superstitions are stupid. Can’t we just go to bed now?”

The rest of his friends and Slim sat there. Quiet. Listening in the woods, along this very, very old trail for any of the old people, or beings, or unknown spirits that may have died along that path. There was a slight breeze through the trees, but nothing more.

“Don’t do that again.” Slim told Maggie. “We go to your churches when you guys get married, we go to your churches on Sunday. You expect us to respect your Christmas, and all your other holidays. We just expect you to respect our ways, especially in our country.”

“Fine, I’m sorry for whistling. I’m sure all the spirits are coming to get us.”

“We don’t joke about that here,” said Slim.

Soda took his hand from Maggie.

“Okay, okay, everyone just calm down. She’s sorry, it’s all done. Nothing happened, we’re good. Just drink the rest of your beer, eat some of those chips we brought with us.”

There was a dog barking in the background. Before Soda could finish what he was saying, they heard four dogs circling the camp. I knew it.

“Leave her here for the offering,” said Sixty angrily.

“Enough! Everyone, get into your tents. Leave some sort of offering outside of it.” Said Slim with authority, getting up and dumping out his can of beer. “No, we’re not going to leave her out here as an offering. Whistling was a mistake. Make sure you’re ready and alert.”

“They’re just coyotes, I’m sure they’ll leave.” Soda said this, but a hint of fear was on his lips.

“She said, sorry for it, we’ll all just go into our tents.”

“Sounds more like wolves to me,” grunted Fender, grinning to his girlfriend, Tess.

"Don't say that!" She hissed at him.

"Tss... I was just jokin." He hawed back.

"Actually, it does sound like wolves." Slim looked around the group. There was a glassy look of fear in everyone's eyes. He took charge again. "Okay, just everyone calm down. They won't do anything to us. It sounds like there's only a couple of them anyway. We'll just do what Soda said. Everyone, let's all get over it. We'll make sure we leave an offering in the morning at the cave, just in case."

The howling and barking got closer. The other girls started getting scared.

"Okay, well, maybe we'll double up on people in the tents tonight." Said Sixty.

"Good idea," said Fender.

"Slim, you can come with Maggie and me," said Soda.

"I don't want to. I'm sure I'll be fine by myself in my own tent." Slim said this a little bit mockingly. "Like I would want to sleep in the same tent as the summoner over there. No thanks, I'll do just fine by myself."

So, the rest of them downed their beers. Slim took a bag of chips with him to his tent. He didn't check or care how they were going to divide the sleeping arrangements. They all went to bed. Nothing happened that night. The barking stopped soon afterwards. But it wasn't going to stay that way.

There was a slight hint of snow on the air. The smell of it was crispy and clear. Fender woke Slim up from outside of the tent with a quick shake.

"Hey buddy, wake up. We're thinking that maybe we'll head back. I think it's going to snow tonight." He whispered. "The winds have changed. Maybe we'll cut it short and head back. We don't want to be stuck out here. There's nothing but dirt roads."

"Alright. Just give me ten minutes and I'll back up," he said.

In their haste to leave, the camp never left their offering to that cave. Only Slim had left his personal offering of a buttless smoke from the day before. The wind could be heard up in the lodgepole pines along the mountain sides. The morning was early and the sun had just cleared the lowest ridge, lighting the morning mist like a heatless blanket. They started to walk back towards the main trail that led to where their trucks were. Everything was fine for the first kilometre or so. But, six kilometres can feel like twelve as soon as someone gets hurt.

Janie tripped over a tree root and bashed her knee into a sharp rock, cutting it wide.

"Oww!" she wailed as she splayed out, bumping into Fender who leaned down and picked her up.

"Shit! You okay?" Fender looked down at the cut, then split the pant leg. "I don't think we have anything we can use to cover this. That's a pretty gnarly gash."

"It's fine... it's fine. We'll be fine." Her boyfriend, Sixty, was distraught. "I have tape and antiseptic shit..."

"I got a clean shirt in my bag," said Soda.

So they quickly wrapped it and continued after a ten-minute stop. Janie was handling it well, but was limping heavily, so the going was slow. The smell of blood was on the air now.

Soon after that point, around 30 minutes after preparing her leg, there was a little bit of snow in the air and the clouds started to obscure the sky. They felt the energy change.

Slim could feel eyes watching them. Many. More than the four they thought they heard last night.

"I think we're being stalked. Those coyotes that we heard last night. Actually, I don't even know if they are coyotes. They could have been wolves for all we know. I think we're being stalked by them."

Seconds after he said that, a twig snapped. They all turned, looking for it. They didn't see it, but everyone was freaked out by now. So Sixty scooped up his girlfriend Janie, and they hauled it. The good thing was, the next kilometre or so was all on flat ground with high visibility. They ran. It was hard to run on the moist ground. It was soft and gave way under their feet, and their packs were heavy and daunting. They made it another kilometre before Sixty almost gave out.

"Okay, everyone. Just give me a minute. I need some water," Sixty panted.

Janie's leg was bleeding profusely at this point. They sat there together, dabbed at it a little bit more. The leg was inflamed and looked angry.

"Are you guys sure we don't have a sewing kit or something? Maybe we should just sew this thing shut or something. It's looking worse and worse, and it hasn't been very long."

As Slim said this to them, immediately around them in the clearing, wolves crept into view, forming almost a perfect circle. One of them was almost completely black. Slim swore he saw it had red eyes. It also appeared that it stood on its hind legs looking at him. The campers all started to scream. Everyone dropped their equipment. Sixty picked up Janie again, and they started to run.

"Sixty, just stop for a second. You're too tired for this. You're starting to slow down."

"Let me carry her," Slim said.

But it was too late. The second they slowed to hand her over, a grey wolf pounced. It took Janie by the leg and dragged her into the woods. She screamed. Sixty tried to follow them, but another wolf came in and bit him on the legs. He fumbled for his knife and dropped it in the tall grass that was already obscured by snow. The rest of the group kept going. Slim tried to grab at the wolf, and it scratched him. He fumbled for his own knife and got it out just in time to stab deep into its shoulder. It yelped and slunk away. The other wolves were chasing after their prey as the campers bolted down the trail.

Slim and Sixty seemed like they were alone.

"Okay, buddy, are you okay?" Sixty was not okay. He was bleeding profusely from several wounds—one of them was gushing high up on his thigh. The wolves knew exactly where to bite, but he was alive. With Slim's help, they could try to make it through the trail. It was a brisk morning, but the adrenaline was making it hot, so Slim took off his coat and wrapped it around his friend, he ripped up his shirt, and wrapped it tightly around the leg that was bleeding the worst. Slim knew that the wolves would be back so they stumbled along the trail after their friends, who were long gone by now.

They could hear growling and barking both behind and in front of them. Pressing forward, they made good distance. But Sixty was becoming more sluggish with every step. They made it back to the woods, still heading in the right direction.

They saw a body—Soda. He was dead. His throat gaped and a thick puddle of blood formed around his head like a halo. They could see every moving bit in there. His eyes stared right at them as they entered the woods. Lifeless and bloody.

"Oh my god. I hope everyone else got away." Slim seethed through breathless gasps.

Not knowing what else to do, they left Soda there and kept going. They stumbled not quite a kilometre more and saw blood, pieces of clothing, a partial hand, tents and equipment strewn about the trail.

There was a marker a little more than halfway up the trail. "Sixty, buddy. We'll wait up there for a minute, okay?

I gotta check your wounds and check our equipment, see if there's anything we can use to help you, to help us, some sort of weapon or something."

Slim walked back a little bit, leaving his friend there with the knife. They were leaving a bloody trail behind them, and he knew that the rest of those wolves would be back for them. He saw one of the bags, ripped and bloody. He opened it and started rifling through it. He found a tarp, and shoved it into his coat. He then saw some lines for tying, and a thick cord of rope, and shoved that into his coat. A couple of dirty metal band t-shirts. Looked like it was Crush's bag. Crush wasn't anywhere to be seen. He was the fastest, so maybe he was able to outrun the wolves. He went to the next bag. Four fingers of a right hand sat lifelessly on top of it. It was Fender's stuff. Fender wasn't anywhere to be seen.

Hopefully, that's a good thing... Slim said to himself, ignoring the partial hand.

He kept rifling through. There was a little bit of hard alcohol in there—some vodka. Well, this might be good to clean those wounds. He grabbed it. He neglected to grab any of the food and probably should have brought the bag with him.

Slim heard a high-pitched yell, like a man and wolf combined. He turned quickly, back behind them on the trail. Again, he saw that black wolf, standing on its hind legs, looking at him. It stood 150 feet behind him. It fell onto all fours and started running at him.

He turned and ran. He went to the marker on the road. Sixty was sitting on the ground leaning against the marker. He was bleeding profusely and was becoming delirious—Slim could tell. Sixty's eyes were glassy and looking out into nothing, not even reacting to Slim or the wolf rushing at them.

"Sixty, hurry, we need to go, that thing is after us."

He grabbed his friend and they began to limp away.

"I can't, my legs hurt so much, just leave me." Sixty painfully wheezed.

"No, I can't leave you, Sixty, we need to go. If I leave you, there won't be anyone left.

"Just do it. Leave that knife for me."

Slim looked at his friend and gave him the knife.

"You'll be okay," he hoped. "Defend yourself. I'll come back for you when I get back to the cars. There's an axe and a compound bow in the car, I'll bring them back. Just stay alive, Sixty." Slim ran.

No more than a minute and a half later, while running and out of breath, he heard Sixty scream. That scream quickly descended into a wet gurgle. And then nothing.

He stopped and looked back. He saw nothing, but heard quick footsteps rushing around him. Because of the clouds and the snow, the morning was overcast. He could no longer see the tops of the mountains. The blowing wind started to pick up. The flakes got bigger and blustery. He looked around him through the woods. At least eight sets of eyes were moving along with him, circling. One set was red. They were following and chasing him, but not trying to attack him for some reason. Slim continued to run, trying to ignore his burning lungs. There was a large outcropping of fallen rocks on the trail up ahead.

He wasn't even halfway back to the cars, he realized. As he approached the large rock cluster he saw another body hidden behind the rocks.

He ran and stopped to take a breath, leaning against a rock. His adrenaline was finally starting to fail him. He looked down at the body. It was Fender. His right hand was bleeding from where the fingers were ripped off. He was gone. The frozen silent scream of fear was etched into his features.

"Oh no. Oh no... oh no..." was all Slim could whisper.

There's only two of them left. Soda and Maggie. There was no sign of them. Their equipment was still with them too.

"Soda! Wait for me!"

He tried to yell out but was too out of breath. It wasn't loud enough. The wind was starting to howl. The snow was blowing into his face, stinging and biting.

"Fender, my friend, I'm sorry. I need to take your coat." He slipped the bloody coat off of him.

It was still warm with his blood.

"Where's your knife?" He searched through his pockets. He found a lighter, but no knife.

"I'll come back for all of you. I will. I promise." He continued on.

The morning was stretching into early afternoon. It was hard to tell, but the light was still in the middle of the sky. Since he was in the mountains, and it was late in the season, there was only about three hours of light left.

He needed to find his friends and make it back to the cars. But he was tired. The wolves were still in pursuit. They were keeping distance but circling continuously. He heard a howl at his back. Too close for comfort. He didn't dare look back at it, but again, it almost sounded like a man.

He crept forward even more. The world was turning white and windy. "Where's the river?" The snow was starting to blind him. Where did this come from? It wasn't even supposed to snow this week.

He stumbled further. Through the howling wind, he could catch the sounds of water. He found the river. Luckily, at this time of year, the river was low and easy to cross. But it still seemed like all the rocks that they had hopped on to get over that trail were now submerged. He had to get wet. He took a moment as the snow stopped and the wind exposed the tops of the nearby mountains. He caught his breath.

Oh, I found the river, he thought. *I'll cross and take a break. I need to. I think I lost them, I think I lost him, I need to find the trail.* He was alone now, out of breath and nearly delirious, his feet hurt, soaking wet. He had to slog through the knee-deep water—freezing cold.

He crossed it but tripped and fell onto the bank, scraping his hands. He turned about, in fear that the wolves would take that opportunity and finish him. He had thought he was alone, but across the river stood four wolves with bloody maws. They waited and just watched him. Up slunk the black wolf with red eyes. It almost seemed to be smiling at him. Slim stumbled to his feet and ran.

'Soda, where are you?" He was mumbling it more to himself than to Soda. He expected that Soda and Maggie were dead by now too. He was alone for all he knew. "Soda, where are you?"

The snow was coming down hard. The jacket wasn't heavy enough to keep him warm, and the blood from it was starting to freeze upon his skin. He took the tarp from his shirt. It was dry and not bloody. He also took the rope and tied the tarp around himself as a way to keep the snow off and keep dry. He would have to use it later as a shelter if he didn't make it back.

The trail was starting to get hard to see with all the snow that was picking up around him. He only had about two kilometres left to walk. Not far for an avid hiker, but too far for a man alone in his fear and grief. For about 10 minutes he heard nothing but wind, saw nothing but snow. He could still see the trail through the trees, but just barely.

He couldn't see footprints up ahead of him. *Soda and Maggie must be gone,* he thought to himself. *They must be dead somewhere.*

He continued. The trail suddenly came to a fork in the road.

"What? I don't, I don't remember this. I don't remember this being here at all." Usually he was good at picking apart his directions and how far he was from where he parked.

"I just need to make it back. Please, where do I go?" He said aloud. He was starting to get very cold now.

He had hiking shoes, but not winter boots.

"Why? How is the snow so deep by now?" It was past the top of his boots. What should have taken him no more than an hour or two was starting to stretch late into the afternoon. He could tell by the light that it was getting late. He took the path to the right.

"This must be it... This feels... This feels... This feels like it should be right." His teeth chattered as he muttered to himself, not actually being sure but needing to make a decision.

He could feel those wolves getting closer. He was the last, so he was next.

He stumbled further. The sunlight faded even faster than he thought it would. He stumbled further, and then he saw fire along the path.

Oh good. I'm so cold. Why is this happening?

He stumbled. He slipped. He fell. As he was trying to get back to his feet, he slipped and fell again. He looked up at that fire from the cold ground. It looked so inviting, barely dancing in the heavy wind. He didn't see anyone tending to it. He focused all on that fire. First crawling, then sliding, he managed to get back on his feet and stumbled towards it.

After what felt like five minutes of braving the wind and the snow, he made it. The wind and snow died down around him immediately. He was in someone's camp. He didn't know where the tent was or who had lit the fire. Just then, out of nowhere, a man walked up. Rugged and old. He was a native and wore a heavy buffalo robe over leather clothing that he couldn't quite see.

Slim, like many of his friends, only knew a little bit of Blackfoot. So, he didn't know if he would be able to communicate with the man, but he tried to talk to him anyway.

"Oki, nisto Slim," He squeaked out.

The man didn't seem bothered by the wind or the snow, and he stood there, rugged, wearing thick buffalo fur, long black, braided hair. Dark eyes.

"It's okay, brother. I speak English, too, you know." He smiled warmly. "Come on, little brother. Come warm yourself by the fire."

Slim looked around them into the trees, trying to catch a glimpse of the wolves.

"What's wrong? Why are you covered with blood?" The wind and snow howled around them, but not amidst them. He was warm in this man's company.

"Here, go sit." The man motioned toward one of two seats. Slim fell into an old wood and leather seat.

"Here, eat some of this. I just hunted it the other day," he said. "Okay, no worries, settle down, brother. So, tell me what's going on."

"I ... uh. ..." Slim couldn't figure out what to say.

"Why are you out of breath? Why are you alone?" He raised his eyebrows toward Slim.

"Can't you see what's around us? The Old Man is angry." Slim sat there for a minute dumbfounded.

"The Old Man River?" The man looked out towards the river.

"No.... The wolf...." Slim's words trailed off and he noticed the wolves again. "Where's your camp? Maybe we should go there. I'll talk to you there. We can't sit out in the open. There are wolves here. They're after me and my friends."

"Oh, it's okay. Calm down." He acted like the wolves weren't even there. "They won't come towards the fire. You sit and tell me."

So, Slim told him this story.

"Holy, that's a lot. Maybe you should leave an offering," he said, matter-of-fact.

Slim looked at him. "I did leave an offering. I told them they needed to leave offerings too." He was feeling cold again.

"Those beings are mad at you and your friends." The man now looked stern. "Something is off. What happened?"

"I told you what happened." Slim was dumbfounded. "What do you mean what happened?"

"What did you find in the cave?" The man threw another log on the fire.

"We found ... just a few knickknacks. We left them there. I left an offering later. There's some paintings in there. There's nothing else.... We left them." Slim was stammering, trying to remember everything.

"Are you sure you left them? Come on, brother," he urged Slim. "Maybe someone else? Maybe one of your friends took something?"

"No.... No, they wouldn't have taken anything. They know not to take anything.

"Do they all know?" The man poked the fire with a stick.

Slim thought back for a moment. He remembered that Maggie had been playing with part of a beaded necklace that they found. He had quickly told her not to play with it. He said that they shouldn't be touching those relics. That they don't know what sort of medicine they have on them. His other friends told her too. But she had been ignorant to those things. She had laughed and tossed it back onto the ground.

"I thought it was pretty, okay. Don't be so bent out of shape. This is just some old stuff. I wasn't going to take it," she had said. But that must be it. Thinking back on that exchange, she was the last one to leave the cave and walk back to their campsite. He knew it then, shivering in the cold. She had taken that necklace with the beading that had four claws on it. They had guessed at the time that they were wolf claws or badger claws or something like it. It was starting to dawn on Slim that he knew exactly what kind of claws they were. They were definitely wolf. As it came back to him, he looked into the man's eyes and the man looked back at him with scorn.

"Now you know. You took something without offering."

"I didn't take it," he said defensively.

"But you didn't check if she had taken it. You need to make an offering in her stead," he said.

"Why don't I just find her? She should be on this trail or the other one. We can find her together. She can make it right."

"Hmm. I think maybe she and your friend made it back to my camp. I think maybe I'd seen them earlier." The man motioned to the trees behind him a ways back.

"Why didn't you tell me that?" Slim was now wary.

"I didn't know if they were with you. They were hysterical and they weren't bloody like you are. They didn't mention anything about anyone else behind them." The man shrugged.

"Soda... Soda didn't... mention that we were being chased by wolves?"

"Ah. All he said was he needed to get back to the truck. Get out of the weather. With him and his girlfriend. I told him that they should come back to my lodge. I have a winter wood lodge just around the corner of that trail. For some reason, I knew that I should make a fire and come out here. And now I know why." He got up from his seat. "To hear your story and to make sure you set it right."

Slim was confused. *Why would his friends talk like... why would his friends act like they didn't exist? When they knew full well that at least a few of them were dead behind them? Were they just going to leave us here?* He thought this all to himself. And then he spoke to the man. "Well, take me back to your lodge. If they're there, then we can... we can make this right. And the wolves will stop pursuing us."

"Hmm. Okay. You can come back to my lodge. But be careful. Your friend and his woman. They don't respect it out here. You shouldn't trust them."

"It's fine. I'm sure they were going to come back for us anyway... it's fine." Slim was stumbling over his own words. "Please, let's just get warm and out of the snow. Our cars are nearby. We can go back there and get help. But I need to get warm and I need to hear what happened to them in the last hour...the last couple of hours...I don't even know how long it's been."

"Okay. Come follow me," the man said.

They walked through the wind and snow, up the trail further. Slim stumbled while the man didn't seem to notice the snow. They rounded a bunch of trees nearby, just high on a crest overlooking the water, there was a very old-looking lodge made of hardy timber. There were racks around the camp for stretching hide. There was one very fresh deer hide on one, stretched and drying by a fire. They went to the door. Slim stopped before he went inside.

"Aren't you coming, friend? Come inside. We'll warm up and give you some more food. We'll sort this out. Make an offering. Those wolves will leave you be." The man motioned to Slim.

"I don't..." Slim couldn't help himself. There was an uneasy feeling about this lodge. "Where are my friends and how come I can't hear them?"

"I don't know, friend. Just go in. I'm sure they're back in there. They're just afraid, so they're quiet. It's okay. We'll find the medicine she took. Put it back. It will be fine, friend."

"Who are you, and what are you doing out here?" Slim couldn't shake the feeling. "Do you just live out here by yourself?"

The man turned and looked at him again.

"Sure, I stay out here most of the time. I was one of the ones who never agreed to live on a reserve." He was trying to talk smoothly to Slim.

Slim thought about what the man had said for a second. *What does he mean by that?* "None of us agreed to live on a reserve. What are you talking about? It doesn't matter anyway."

The wording was weird, but he was getting cold and it was getting snowy. He shook off this weird feeling of dread.

"It's okay, friend. Just come in."

Slim took a couple steps and went into the door. He hovered by the door, just inside. It was warm. Just like a traditional lodge. Everything inside was circular, with the fire in a fireplace in the middle—an old, old stone and clay fireplace. There was a shuttered window and no other light than the fireplace. A simple sleeping area was on the back side of the fireplace and the kitchen area was closer to the door. There was food boiling in a pot. But his friends weren't there.

"I thought you told me they were here." Slim narrowed his view at the man.

"Oh, they came. Don't worry about them. Let's see if she left that offering for us." He smiled and sat at the handmade wood table.

Slim went to the boiling pot of soup. Something told him to look inside of it. It smelled delicious. Fresh meat. He fought the urge and didn't take a look in the pot. Probably the same venison that he saw earlier.

"Okay, na'pi, just sit down at that table there. We'll talk about it. Warm up. Maybe your friends just went outside to look for you. They'll be back." The man took up a couple of bowls and spooned the soup into them.

"No. I need to go get help for my friends. The cars are not far, I have to get my other two friends and call the cops." He was getting a bit foggy.

Oh, it smelled good. They woke up with a start that morning, so they never actually ate food. All he'd had was a little bit of cooked venison from earlier. He sat there, mouth watering. A queer feeling came back to him but his stomach growled so he shook it off again. He started to eat the food, slurping at the broth. It tasted so good and it was warming him up. He was still wet and cold. But again, that feeling of dread crept up onto him. So, he looked at the man. Looked him up and down. He hadn't noticed before but, the man was dressed in clothes not of this century. He looked like he was from at least the late 1800s—like what his people looked like at the signing of the treaty. A cowboy hat, earrings, lots of beaded jewellery, mixed with traditional type of clothing and regalia.

More questions came to Slim. He was about to ask the man. Then he heard howling around the lodge outside. Howling, barking, and screaming. It sounded like more than a hundred wolves out there. That couldn't be right.

It was only a small pack after them. The man didn't seem fazed by them. He didn't even react to the howls, just kept eating his soup. Slim dropped the wooden bowl, it splashed and almost rolled off the table. He could hear them getting closer. Afraid, he got up quickly and pushed the bowl right off the table, and onto the ground.

"I'm sorry..."

"It's alright na'pi. I'll clean it." The man just smiled and sat back in his chair. "Just sit down and relax. They can't get us in here."

"I don't know what's happening..."

Just then, Slim looked down at the broth that had pooled on the wood slats on the ground. The meat was peculiar. It didn't look like venison. Slim had eaten a lot of venison in his life. But that did not look like venison. He looked down and picked up a piece of the meat. He cringed as he brought it closer to his face to get a good look. There were no open windows in the lodge, just the fire. So, it was dim, and the fire danced.

He couldn't see very well. Then he understood what he was looking at. It was a tongue. A human tongue. He looked at the other pieces of meat, and there were five tongues in his bowl. He gasped. Almost cried.

"What is this? These look like human tongues." He asked that question out loud. Almost to himself more than to the man. He looked over at him.

The man sat there. Not quite a smile. Not quite a sneer. "They made their offerings. It's time for you to make yours." He chewed on a piece of meat.

"What?" Slim dropped the tongue, and he looked at the man. "No, I need to leave."

He went to the door of the lodge. He tried to open it. "Let me out. I made my offering."

"And that is why you are alive. It's not enough."

"What do you mean it's not enough?"

"You need to be able to teach the people who come here that they need to respect this place, to respect these teachings and this knowledge. The Old Ways are to be honoured. You are to teach them that lesson." The man gathered the tongues. "So, you need to give one more offering."

"But I... are you expecting me to give my tongue?" The howls grew with the rushing wind outside.

"No. I'm expecting you to give your life." The man stood and started to put the tongues on a string.

"What? What are you...? Who are you?" Slim was now trembling.

"You are to be here forever. You are the new spirit of this place. I have been here a long time. I am the rising wolf, and that is my pack. But now my waiting is over."

As the man said this to Slim, his face morphed and changed. His clothing fell from him, and he turned into the black wolf with red eyes. Standing on his hind legs.

"I am old. That is my pack. They need a new leader. And you... need to warn everyone who comes here that they can't just take. That they need to give offerings. Look. This is now yours."

"Look at what?"

"Look there at the fire." Rising Wolf pointed with his paw.

Slim looked at the fire, and inside of it not burning was the necklace. The jewellery that Maggie had taken. Its four wolf claws were there. The wolf fell onto its four legs, walked to the fire, put its head in the fire without being burnt, and grabbed up the necklace. Then he put the necklace into Slim's hands.

"Your offering is your tongue. It is also your body. Your tongue to tell people—all new comers and interlopers—the truth of this place. It is holy. You cannot disrespect it.

And your body. You accepted coming into my lodge. You've been told that you don't follow beings that you don't know are men into their lodges. Their medicine will take you. My medicine has taken you. You are now mine." His voice growled low and deep. "I am the Rising Wolf. Now I go to be among the ancestors. You! You are to stay."

Slim stopped being scared. The howling outside stopped. The wind stopped. It was completely still. The fire crackled and the necklace clicked in Slim's hand.

"Will you give this offering? Or will I take your tongue and eat your body? I'm giving you a gift. Will you take it? Or not?"

Slim looked at the necklace and then he put it on.

"I give you a new name; 'The Wolf Who Stays.'" Rising Wolf nodded approvingly. He then pushed Slim towards the fire where sweetgrass incense burned.

Rising Wolf then gathered the tongues into his mouth, but did not eat them. He walked to the door, kicked it open and walked out to his pack to give them the tongues. He was never to be seen by mortal eyes again. That would be Slim's—The Wolf Who Stays—fate. Never to make it home. It was good that he was single and hadn't settled down. That wasn't to be his life. He was to stay here and to warn people to stay on the trail and give offerings when knowledge is bestowed.

Give offerings to the ancestors and the beings who bestow knowledge and blessings. For the wolf will take your tongue as your offering to them if you do not observe the natural law. Just watch.

Or his pack will come for you.

"I'm not a murderer.
I am not a murderer,"
he thought. Not knowing
what to do, he drove.

4

DEAD HED

Cary Thomas Cody

"GOD, WHAT HAPPENED HERE?" A coroner said as he walked up to a corpse, seemingly regretting his career choice. He held a bandana to his mouth, and it looked as if he might vomit.

A Bureau of Indian Affairs officer was the first to the scene. "From what I can tell, the poor bastard stepped out of his Mack truck, probably to take a piss, forgot to put it in park and it rolled right over him."

"What a way to go," said the coroner, having seen many gruesome deaths over the years, hardly as bloody as this. "Gah, looks like he got hit by all 18 wheels. Do you have an identification on him?

"Affirmative. Jerry Hedfield, 43 years old. A truck driver from up north. His CDIB says he's from the Crow Agency in Montana, 50 percent blood quantum. No story or information on why he ended up on our Rez, trucks usually don't drive through this area.

"Woah, look at his face! What in the world made him do that?"

The coroner looks closer, a mere foot away from his bloody, bloated face. The last scare of the corpse's life permanently petrified in his eyes.

"It's... twisted. His face I mean. Bells Palsy possibly?" The coroner pulls back and looks at the officer. "Have you ever seen anything like this?"

The BIA officer stepped back, now noticing animal tracks by the corpse. "When I was growing up we called it 'crooked face.' Yeah, I've seen it, but not in many years."

Jerry Hedfield was catching up to a traffic jam, a sea of red taillights as far as he could see. "Breaker 1-9, Breaker 1-9. Anyone out there know what's holding up traffic? Over." He held his CB radio in anticipation for a response.

"Big wreck up on around mile marker 100, might wanna find a detour there, partner. Over," said a female voice on the radio.

"I heard that, yep, yep." Jerry responded. "Say, what's your call sign there, Darlin'?"

"Don't call me Darlin'. You can call me Jane Doe. Who am I speaking to? Over."

"I'm Jerry, but my handle is Dead Hed."

"Dead Hed? Does it mean anything in particular?"

"Just an old nickname from my Army days, that's all. Over."

"Well, Dead Hed, you might wanna head down 58 South if you still can make the exit, this semi is flipped over and it's going nowhere fast," said the female trucker, Jane Doe.

Jerry held his brand new 1985 United States road atlas open and traced it with his finger. "I can see the route. But hey, sure you don't want to hop in my truck and take a ride with me?" he said, throwing a Hail Mary to this attractive voice on the radio. Truckers weren't the most gentleman-like on the radios, and Jerry Hedfield specifically was not one for romantic gestures.

"With a name like Dead Hed, I wouldn't be caught dead in your truck. Besides, I already took the exit, I'm a few miles ahead of you Dead Hed."

"Ouch, I can take a hint. Thanks for the intel, Ms. Doe. Over."

Jerry saw the string of red lights ahead of him, and just before he met them, he hit his turn signal and made an exit on 58 South.

He couldn't stop thinking about the female voice that he met on the CB. It's not common to meet lady truckers on the road, so he reached out to start a conversation. There's not much else to do on these highways. "Jane Doe, are you there? Over." He heard static. "Jaaaaane." He must be out of range, that or Ms. Doe is ignoring him.

Static.

He and his 18-wheel rig drove southeast, just passing a sign that said "Entering Kiowa-Comanche-Apache Reservation."

Jerry was drafted in the Army the second he grabbed his diploma in 1965. He didn't really have many plans in life, so he didn't argue much when his dad handed him his draft letter. He basically was dropped into battle without any real firearm training. The most experience he had with a gun was when they were kids and played Cowboys and Indians with cap guns and plastic bows and arrows. Except, since he grew up on an Indian reservation, everyone only wanted to play Indians and Indians.

Fighting the Viet Cong was basically that, Cowboys and Indians. Except this time, he was the cowboy, the Calvary riding into battle to slaughter the savages. If only it was that simple.

He was dropped right into the jungle around zero dark thirty. Eighteen years old, never even having laid with a woman. Bullets whizzing past his face, army-crawling through the trenches, thankful that each time a bullet landed on flesh it wasn't his. Until it was. A year and six months after being taken from his home and having had a gun placed in his hands, Jerry Hedfield, or "Dead Hed" as his platoon called him, was found shot and bleeding to death in a field. His entire platoon was assassinated, and he was the only survivor.

Jerry was awarded a Purple Heart and medically discharged from the military. He survived the war. The term "survived" was generous. The boy who went into the Army was not the man that walked out. He came back with more than a medal. He came home with a load of Shell Shock. He still has nightmares of those Viets prowling through the jungle.

He just wanted to make his dad proud. Instead, he came back to the good ol' United States being labeled a woman and child killer. His dad couldn't even look him in the eyes anymore. *I was just following Uncle Sam's orders,* he thought. Sure, he did some things he wasn't proud of, but dammit, he did it for his country. And they called him a murderer.

Bastards.

"Breaker Breaker 1-9, Jane Doe are you there?" He held the CB tight, hoping for a response. Static rang through the radio. He sure would like some company tonight, he thought, even if it's just a female companion on the radio.

"Well, there he is! Hey Handsome, it's Jane Doe here."

Jerry had a little bit of a stomach drop. She called him handsome. Was she flirting? Suddenly wide awake he responded. "I... was hoping to hear from you, Darlin.' Any Charlies on this route?" He said, trying to keep the conversation alive while he waited through the static of the radio for her response.

"I told you not to call me Darlin.' And negative, clear sailing all the way through the reservation, Handsome."

Jerry hadn't felt the touch of a woman in a coon's age. Well, that's if you didn't count the filthy Lot Lizards at truck stops in the desert. Twenty bucks will get you some action, but 50 bucks will get you some "Boom Boom." But it ain't like the passion behind love making. Just the fact she called him Handsome sent a large amount of blood flow down his trousers.

Lacking a response, he just asked the general trucker questions.

"Jerry, you do know I'm flirting with you right?" Jane said through radio waves.

"I... uh it's been a while since that's happened, to be honest." Jerry said.

"How about I make you an offer? I'm feeling very lonely tonight, and I don't want to spend the evening by myself again. I could use some sexual healing, if you know what I mean. I am actually from around these parts and could find us a place to meet if you'd be interested. Do you copy?"

Without hesitation, he grabbed the CB and said, "Name the time and place. Over." Static rang through the radio, and suddenly he realized he was out of range to get a response.

He thought to himself... *Are you fucking kidding me? Can I catch a break for God's sake.* "Jane, are you there? Do you copy? Over." More static. "Where should we meet? Over." And there was still no response.

Jerry drove South, the disappointment evident by how aggressive he was behind the wheel. The feeling in his loins was one he hadn't felt for a long time—just the idea that a woman wanted to have sex with him instead of him paying for it, Jesus. He hadn't even seen this woman and had no idea what she looked like and she still had him a wreck like this. He didn't care what she looked like, honestly. He wasn't even sure if she was actually a woman, but he was lonely enough to want to find out.

The last time he had sex was months ago. Driving through Arizona, or New Mexico or one of those desert places, he picked up a Lot Lizard. It wasn't hard to do, and he was never proud of it. But it was just easy. He had gained quite a bit of weight during his trucker tenure, and he never really was the most handsome guy, even though Jane seemed to think he was just by the sound of his voice. But a man has needs, even if it's from some hooker at a truck stop. At least he hadn't resorted to asking for sexual favours from other men truckers, he'd seen the holes in the side of gas station bathroom stalls and knew what they were for. *There ain't a woman on the other side of that stall, partner,* he thought.

No, the last time was the last time he was going to pay for sex. A cute young Indian girl, Pueblo or Navajo probably. Couldn't have been more than 18, and no younger than 18 he thought, lying to himself. He invited her to his truck, even though she wasn't the most attractive. She was very skinny, short hair, and very timid. She had performed her duties, made him feel loved, and tried to leave the truck with more than her $20 payment. She had his entire wallet.

Jerry saw red, and the next thing he knew she was bleeding and knocked out in the cab of his truck. "I'm not a murderer. I am not a murderer." He thought. Not knowing what to do, he drove. He dumped her about 20 miles off in the desert, off some random dirt road.

He honestly thought she was dead, but as he was leaving her, he heard the faintest whimper. *That's just in my head.* But the deed had been done, he was leaving her in the desert in the dead of the summer.

He had not hit a woman since Vietnam, and thought those days were surely over. He thought he was a changed man. As he was driving away from the young sex worker, he tried not to look in the rear-view mirror, but he glanced, and he thought he saw her running towards him. He told himself that was all in his head. Maybe this whole nightmare was just that, a nightmare.

Suddenly his CB radio lit up. "Dead Hed, do you copy? Are you not interested in meeting with me?" Jane Doe called out.

"Yes absolutely, where? Over." Jerry was ecstatic, maybe his CB wasn't out of range after all.

"I told you three times already silly, let's meet at the ol' truck stop off the junction of 19 and 58. Meet me in the women's restroom, I'll make sure it's empty and we have a warm spot to fool around. Over."

"I copy. You know, we could just hook up in one of our trucks? Over."

"No thank you. I don't get into strange men's trucks. Besides, doesn't a little public display of affection turn you on a little?" The trucker with the caller sign Jane Doe responded, alluringly.

"Women's restroom at the ol' truck stop, I'll find it. Say, do you need me to bring anything?" He asked, assuming maybe she'd want a bottle of Tito's, or perhaps a condom.

"Just bring yourself, Handsome. I'm gonna be in there warming myself up. Don't take too long."

And with that, Jerry's whole body was full of shivers. He was going to get laid by this insanely hot woman, or at least he was imagining how hot she was by the sound of her voice. Jerry put his foot on the pedal and drove as fast as he could to find this truck stop.

Jerry arrived at the truck stop. It was… decrepit. But somehow the dim yellow phosphorescent lights were still functioning. Not exactly where he envisioned meeting with a lady. She had given the impression it was a functional gas station, did she not? But sure enough, there was another 18-wheeler there in the lot that he could only assume was hers. What he couldn't tell from the darkness though, was that semi-truck hadn't been driven in many years. He put a mint in his mouth, smelled his breath and thought it was passable. Was he seriously considering going into this dark, desolate truck station in the middle of the night for some sex? Yes, without a question he was. He needed it. He had to have it. And it wasn't just sex, it was going to be love making.

Before he exited the truck, he could see a dark, petite figure of a woman walking towards his truck coming from inside the gas station. He watched in curiosity as the lady, who he could now see was wearing a Native American shawl knocked on the passenger side window.

"Hey, Dead Hed, are you just going to sit in there all night or are you coming inside to keep me company?"

Jerry sat there in stunned disbelief. Nothing was normal about tonight, from the wreck on the highway to the flirting on the CB radio, and now this gorgeous woman who now stands on the sidestep of his truck. He rolled down the window, each hand crank of the window lever revealed more of her beauty. He was speechless.

She stared at him with beautiful, inviting, yet familiar eyes. "Wow, you really are handsome. I'm getting lucky tonight." She said without breaking eye contact. "I'll be in the women's restroom, don't make me start without you." And she stepped off the running board of the truck with the sound of her high heels on the steel of the truck steps and walked seductively back to the gas station.

The parking lot was deteriorated, full of cracked asphalt and gravel. He made his way towards the restroom. Each step with his alligator skin boots crunched the dirt. He made his way around the side of the truck stop, and sure enough the women's restroom was unlocked. He slowly cracked the door open and looked inside. "Hello?" he said with low confidence.

"I thought you'd never make it," said a voice in the very back handicap stall. Underneath the stall dividers he could see a little mattress laid on the ground, or possibly just blankets she laid out for them both to lie down. The restroom had one flickering light bulb above the sink, sort of a strobe-like effect setting the mood.

Jerry waited at the bathroom door, now hesitant to move any further. "This isn't exactly what I had in mind, Ms. Doe." He waited for a response, but none came. He just stared at the dirty gas station bathroom stall. At this point he could cut his losses, make a beeline for the truck and drive off. But this opportunity didn't come often. His curiosity caused him to see what was behind "door number three!"

Jerry opened the stall door and saw Jane give him the "come here" motion with her pointer finger. She was unbelievably gorgeous. By far the most beautiful woman that has ever given him the light of day. She grabbed him by his face and pulled him in. For a second, her lips hovered over his, just their warm breath colliding before she laced lips with his. He could live here forever, the most wonderful kiss he had ever experienced.

The woman laughed and pulled back. The faint flicker of the sink light revealed her new face. Jerry grabbed his chest and fell back. He was suddenly paralyzed with fear. The woman he went with into the stall was not the woman standing in front of him anymore.

"Who… the hell are you?" Jerry said as he scooted away, wiping his lips clean of the saliva this seemingly hundred-year-old woman left on him.

"You know who I am." The woman said laughing, and he kept backing up slowly out of the stall towards the door of the rest room. His arm kept clenching his chest. Was he having a heart attack? No, he'd experienced this before. In the jungle he froze in fear while a dozen of his platoon brothers were shot to death in the trees next to him under his watch while they slept. This was the same feeling, a paralysis induced by fear.

The woman laughed and slowly stepped out of the stall. The "clop clop" of what he thought were high heels on the bathroom tile were not that at all. As she stepped closer, the flickering yellow light revealed her true form.

It revealed that her feet were not feet at all. They were hooves.

Clop, clop, clop.

"No, no, no." Jerry pleaded. The hideous, ancient, shawl-wearing woman in front of him inched closer towards him. Her eyes were as black as night, and he saw a mouth full of rotted, stained teeth when she smiled devilishly at him. He scooted back against the door, and she proceeded towards him. Each step closer revealed more of her hideous features.

With a supernatural strength that he could not explain, she brought down one of her hooves in a stomp on his leg that shattered his femur, followed by five or six more lightning-fast stomps on his legs, torso, and pelvic region. Jerry screamed in pain, incapacitated by not only a panic attack, but now a broken leg and some internal bleeding. He used all his strength to army-crawl out of the restroom, now on the cracked concrete and gravel-ridden parking lot of the truck stop.

"Do you know I am?" The hideous, hoof-footed woman asked.

Still crawling slowly, Jerry answered. "You're the Deer woman." He said, whimpering like a dog hit by a car. "I heard stories about you... as a kid." He could see his truck, maybe 50 feet away. If he could get to his truck, he could use the CB radio to call for help and maybe this nightmare would be over. Each inch he moved was agony.

She slowly walked next to him as he crawled into the parking lot. "How about now?" She asked. Jerry looked up and saw her face was now the face of the young hooker he abandoned in the desert a few months prior. Except her face was dehydrated, lips cracked and bleeding, and eyes bloodshot and sunburned.

She looked the same way it looked the second she died in the 120-degree desert. "That's right. I'm also Samantha, the 14-year-old girl you dumped in the New Mexico desert. My parents are still looking for me. Did you know that? The highway patrol found my body, but there wasn't enough left to identify me. I'm forever a Jane Doe. Do you have any idea what it feels like to be eaten alive by a hundred thousand fire ants?"

He did not know that. He remembered walking past missing posters at truck stops across the nation, but never once thought to himself, "that is truly awful for them." Gravel filled his fingers as he crawled and pulled the earth towards him, inching towards the salvation of the truck.

"I am also Anh, the woman that you executed in Vietnam with a bullet to my head. Did you know I left behind two baby boys? They never knew a life without war thanks to what your people did to us." Jerry didn't want to look up, but out of the corner of his eye he could see what he saw in his nightmares ever so frequently, a woman with a hole in her face where her left eye used to be, blood rushing down her face and a hole in the back of her skull that used to hold her brains in place.

"Please… let me go. I'll never hurt a woman again, I'll go to church, I promise I'll be good." He pleaded.

"That's what you said to your ex-girlfriend, who you left with double black eyes isn't it?" The Deer Woman responded.

"So, what are you going to do, stomp me to death? That's what you do right?" His vision was tunneled, his only goal was to reach his truck and call for help. He continued to crawl, dragging his useless, broken leg behind him while now coughing up blood.

"No, that's too good for you." The Deer Woman responded, and walked away.

So... close. Jerry thought as he crawled, not realizing he hadn't heard from the Deer Woman in the past minute or so. *Is... She gone*? He thought again, crawling through the parking lot like he did the Vietnamese jungle. "She was just in my head. She was just in my head." He survived 'Nam, he could survive this.

Then he was blinded by his own headlights, and he heard the familiar sounds that he's heard almost every day for the past twenty years of his life. The 600-horsepower engine of his truck roaring to life. The hiss of the pistons, and the smell of the diesel fuel that still always reminded him of riding the school bus as a kid. He heard the truck change gears and it started slowly rolling forward.

"What are you doing!? Get out of my truck!" He yelled with the little energy he had, almost blacking out due to the pain. He was able to muster the last bit of fury he had left and crawl away, as fast as he physically could. Each crawl was a pathetic attempt to survive a second longer.

His truck was coming toward him slowly, he suddenly knew what deer felt like in the headlights right before their deaths. He flipped over on his back, accepting his fate.

"You bitch," — and then the truck struck him.

The smile of the old woman behind his steering wheel was the last thing he'd ever see.

The Bureau of Indian Affairs officer and the coroner stood over the corpse. "Remind me, where have you seen any thing like this?" asked the coroner.

The BIA officer stepped back while brushing away the hoof prints from the gravel with his boots. He had seen similar homicides just like this and knew what had happened. "Like I said, it was a long time ago."

"Okay. Well, what should I put in my report about what happened?" questioned the coroner, taking Polaroids as he talked.

"The poor bastard stepped out to take a piss, forgot to put his truck in park, and ran himself over. Nothing more to see here," the BIA officer stated, before the CB radio sprang to life in the cockpit of the semi-truck once again.

"Breaker 1-9… Dead Hed, do you copy?"

"I offer him a taste of
my flesh and he refuses
to eat it. don't waste this...
the gravity of this moment"

5

THE TÁLTOS

Jessica Theroux

BORN with a complete set of beautiful white teeth, a startling baby. Black hair, white teeth. Breast-feeding was a nightmare for her mother. In fact most things that should have been simple and sweet were extreme and wrought with strife when it came to mouse. People whispered. She was wiry, lithe, skin stretched over impressive bones. like a baby elk ambling over obstacles. Human like. Clean, no superfluous details. Onlookers hesitated, no cooing or baby talk, silent prayers.

Taken when she was young. Word spread. The doctor said she was sick. Three days she was gone, like Odin or Christ. She came back more quiet, more healthy, more strong. Her new scars were overlooked, friends and family reassured themselves that she had been sick and now she was better.

With mouse, days passed quickly. She would mutter to herself, along she played from sun up to sun down, make potions in the mud with berries and leaves. She was happy by herself. She was never by herself. Always dancing, singing, songs and movements of joy and pain also, tumultuous and sensuous. The spirits clung to her like flames that never burnt up. Even from a distance, adults and children and animals all fell under her spells she would weave from the dandelion seeds and notes from deep within her, from somewhere else.

Her teeth grew, she grew, the conversations with the animals deepened. Her mother fell ill, she'd heal her with her concoctions from the garden, she'd braid her grandmother's hair with her spider-like fingers; just like braiding dandelions. She learned to make her own clothes, flourished with flowers, or with magic to seal the garments with love.

She grew quickly. Then came school and shoes. School children spoke very differently, not the languages of the plants or the earth. Strange laughter, jeering, subtext that the magpies never use. She learned to talk to herself, inside her head.

révūlessel rēvülök.

I am ecstatic, in a trance

In the uncomfortable seat, she would travel in her mind. The teachers didn't know where she went. She wasn't rude; but she answered questions only to herself. She learned easily. She loved art, she loved prayer, she loved learning about humans and science, and math and the beauty of the world around her. She couldn't understand the resistance from the other students. In the halls they'd push and steal, and curse—evil curses on each other. She tried to blend into the taupe walls lest the evil be turned on her.

In moments, her heart reached out. She could see connections being made by the children—tenuous and nuanced like stretched sinew, or spider webbing in wind. Her heart pulled.

Her teeth grew, her breasts grew, skin stretched over fat and muscle now, not just bone. Stretch marks deepened, new scars. If she stooped to pick up a pencil, eyes slipped into the cracks between her clothes and her body. Loose collars and cuffs did not guard her. She learned to lower herself at the knees not the hips. Most of the time.

The gaze of the owl or the squirrel never felt like this. Nervous, unspoken words between quiet moments. She understood while pretending not to. Like keeping answers to the questions to herself. She now had wealth, a bargaining power of some kind: jewels and gemstones. People around her were greedy.

She was frightening. They used baby talk and cooing to ease their fears. She played along, to ease their fears.

Her laugh grew, unnatural, piercing. If she laughed, she thought they'd think she was happy. A veil. Her dad was irritated by it, it hurt his ears. The first lie, she told to him. The lies that laughed from her mouth hurt him, camouflage. Even alone, she spoke to herself out loud less and less, she made fewer potions from earth. She didn't braid her grandmother's hair. Spider fingers were put to new uses.

Haj, regõ rejtem.

I conjure with magic.

She conjured new magic.

Their wants and needs, she subtly obliged, lined up in droves. It started in schoolrooms and stairwells and then more blatant; in basements and bathrooms and alleyways; from sun down to sun up. She would be out in the moonlight, casting spells, revealing flesh and truths for payments of sorts, dancing between lies. Heavy work. Her heart pulled.

Feelings grew in all directions. Pain mingled with desire and regret and mania. Manic to connect. Hysteric. Hysterical. This is not what she remembered. This world was new. Her world of childhood magic was all truth, clean, no superfluous details—ancient, wise, honourable and integral. Roots growing down, branches growing up. This world was all nuanced lies, stories built on top of crooked stories. It was a shaky world; a card castle world. Chased by whispers down halls. Lies wrapped around her and kept her insulated. Amidst all of this, she wasn't able to decipher the truths trying to teach her lessons that slipped between the lies. She was hacking parts of herself off and they were eating it up. She fed them willingly.

She wanted to be truly wanted, to be seen and felt and connected with, not just gobbled up. But she blinded herself to these vulnerabilities and tried to play cool, ignoring how each of them would leave once they had their fill. Grades stayed high, family were for the most part kept happy, if not totally confused. She had always been different… she was coming apart, inner planets spiralling out, knocked from pathways set long ago. She was losing.

> her teeth grew, her laugh grew, when she let it rip, you could see her extra teeth that had grown in. They weren't looking at her teeth.

She went on to further her studies; Anthropology, Philosophy, History, English. New people, she thought she would meet people like her, but she didn't. How could she? She was cloaked in thick veils. No one could see her. She got mad—violent rages would set in and she thought that these people were just a new set of lies and she would find different ways to forget she was alone.

There was something ancient in that practice too, a genetic encoding that pulled her to succumb to actions without consequence. An excuse to not grow, to not look at the truths. She worshipped the gods that would die at 27. Ignore reality and drift off. Fissuring and splitting like rivers flowing down rock face. She would narrate her own story in her head and she told it condescendingly. She would mock herself and her decisions, but in her histrionic frenzies she would fall through traps and hands and labyrinthine trails all over again.

She lied to herself as well as everyone else and so the cycle would continue. Finding her way home each night, she would start the process all over again. Music would softly whisper to her, from the owl and nightjar, like stars shining just enough light. Sonic breadcrumbs, they would sing her path. But the distractions would amplify her lies and she would end up further away—regret and pain of that deceit would keep the distractions flowing and so it went. Singing to find respite, the sun coming up to show her the truths, and the moon casting lunacy on a terrible cycle.

In quiet moments, amidst this chaos, when thinking of her core, she knew she had lessons to share, she wanted to teach, something inside her kept her walking forward. The fire was not completely snuffed out, but her veils were beginning to restrict air. She kept going to school, a school built by humans, but there were truths inside. She felt them. There was decency and hope buried within a casing of intricate and entrenched power structures. She kept breaking parts of herself off to fit into different holes and feed people along the way. She was coming apart, she didn't know how much more she had to give and then one day, out of the blue, she was taken.

word spread that she was sick. three days.
where had she gone?

Spirited away by a witch. a *boszorkāny, léleklátó asszony*, a seeing woman, a táltos like me, but stronger, the earth herself. The smell of fur. Wooden beads braided into her hair. The clacking as we flew, an ancient, syncopated rhythm. Held by familiar, sinewy arms, paper skin, spider-like fingers. Blackened teeth smiling. Matted locks flailing, linen and fur wrapping around me. It would have seemed like a while to walk, my brain trying to hold onto reality, but the journey blurred together. A different reality was setting in. Sweet grasses danced below us; winds licked our exposed skin. We were one being, flying above the earth, below the sky westwards.

The woman's home was hidden away in the mountains, pine, and sod. Rag and bone. We sat by the fire, in the hearth, in the thick quiet, amidst the howling coyote and the chirping crickets.

I breathed slow, heavy, the incense and spices in the air. Marjoram, paprika, garlic. Handed a ceramic bowl, slowly and with great effort, I swallowed a sludge that tasted like earth and organs and ancient knowledge, honey, and caraway. Everything began to float. Gravity dissipated. Twisting vapour trails and smoke rivulets ringed the room. There was a thumping in my ears. The old woman was laughing. It wasn't a false or forced laugh. It was a guttural thing, from the womb of the earth. The roots of the home shook. The colours blurred and pulsed around her. Slowly I peered through thick air, slowly from side to side and slowly realized my skin was peeling from my body.

Dancing like ribbons in the smoky air. Like peeling a carrot, my skin hung around me. I began to laugh. Blood droplets, anti-gravity bubbled around me like water in oil air. The old woman swam through the space towards me and started pulling at my muscles. They tugged briefly and gave way, like cleaning a turkey at Christmas. Biceps, triceps, calf muscles, ass. Torn musculature mingling with smoke and blood, and skin and laughter.

Once my skin and muscles were free, dancing around me, I noticed the woman going for my organs, her spider fingers delicately handling my intestines, pulling them like sausages hanging them over her shoulders, liver next, the poor beast, lungs, what did i need them for? I thought my brain must still be kept safe in my skull, but what did I know anymore?

My heart
the thumping of my heart
in the old woman's paper hands
deafening
she licked it
tasting the lies and the hidden truths both
the whole room pulsed
my whole body surrounding us

You have one chance left to use this well
or I'm eating it
you've been given such a gift
you're wasting it

She tossed the heart towards the fire
we two women paused in space, hung in air

heart on fire
Centre
nerves electricity buzzing
fairy lights around the room
the woman wasn't laughing any more
everything was quiet except the heart
the women the fire the flesh the organs and blood the obscenity of the normalcy of that moment
Heart of fire

lungs slowly breathing in the moment from somewhere across the room

she plucked the heart from the centre of the room
and handed it to me
my bone fingers holding my beating flaming heart
she next handed me a needle and thread
                get to work.
it took a long time
the night must have come and gone and come again
it was harder work putting things back in place
my consciousness was struggling between
the airy moments before and completing a task so
concrete
Heart first
i pulled the needle through the meat of my heart and
hung it perfectly in the centre of my chest.
a magpie nest among empty Autumn branches
it pulsed and flamed and the fire didn't hurt me and
the needle didn't hurt
much
next my lungs pulled around my heart
clicked my rib cage back in place
the liver—it was pinker now—and my guts pulled
together with ease.
i pulled my nerves together, carefully weaving them
through my inner spaces
muscle, fat, and flesh
I packed the meat back on as best i could
by the end the stitches in my skin became unruly with
fatigue
more scars
but i finished

the woman was gone
the sun was pouring like melted butter through the cracks in the house
dust was the only thing hanging in the air now.
i was naked
but i was whole
i started to walk home

the ground felt startling under my toes
new sensations
crisp
the wind touched every part of me and i shivered in the knowing
the fever was gone and my brain was fully awake.
my heart pulsed
On my journey
Feeling invincible at first
and then betrayed
Stones and sharp rocks began to slice my raw skin
fresh seams

I stumbled a few times, woozy from the days before

i kept getting up, slower and slower.
knees bleeding now

the last time i fell, i thought that was it.
hunger had now taken over
and thirst
the fresh air had turned cold
i realized i never really knew loneliness until now

a hand comes in to view
these hands were not spider like, or papery

he was strong

i go to take his hands to pull myself up

only practiced in my lies, i start spewing them
about how I came to be there, how i found myself so beat up,
my old lying laugh is back, punctuating my tales
my hands are weak, not because of the events that have recently transpired
but they are weak with deceit

I lose grip

he's there to help

But he only deals in truth

he drops his hands he's neither disappointed nor impressed
i look up into his eyes.

This giant of a man, ocean eyes
infinite
I can hear his heart beating from where I sit.

He doesn't smile, he kneels
without moving his perfect lips
i hear

Truth

I laugh and the laugh is lies and he shakes his head and my heart is thumping loud in my ramshackle body

I offer him a taste of my flesh
and he refuses to eat it
    don't waste this
the gravity of this moment
where once everything was floating
Jupiter
intense gravity pulling everything into reality

he sees me
through all my veils
he sees me
he knows me
he remembers me
tears rolling down my cheeks
salt stinging the fresh stitches
my teeth shining
in my first true smile
since i was a kid
he's patient
he's kind
he's waiting
he is of the earth
and the skies and the water and
his words are the words of magpies
his shoulders are mountains
and he has a fire in his heart
so bright it shines through
his fingernails

did you know i was born with a full set of teeth?

"Then, the tracks stopped.
There was nothing,
it was as if it
turned into a bird
and flew off."

6

WISDOM OF NAHGANNE SASQUATCH OF THE NORTH

Raymond Yakelaya

SASQUATCH, or Nahganne as we call them, are more than legends—they are real beings with powers shrouded in mystery. Among the Sahtu Dene People of the North, Nahganne are understood to be intelligent, emotional creatures with their own language and medicine power. Their presence is not just physical; it is spiritual, woven into the fabric of our stories and histories.

Our connection to them may stretch back to the last Ice Age, some 25,000 years ago, when both Nahganne and our ancestors crossed the land bridge from Siberia to this continent. For millennia, our two species have shared this land, living side by side in ways both known and unknown.

Yet despite this longstanding relationship, much about Nahganne remains a mystery. Their ways are elusive, their purpose unclear. Through the stories handed down by our Elders and the experiences of those who have encountered them, we continue to seek answers. Where are Nahganne most concentrated? What do they eat? What is their role in the natural world, and what lessons might they hold for us? These are questions we ask as we step into a realm that blurs the lines between the seen and the unseen, the known and the unknown.

For the Sahtu First Nations people, spirituality is not confined to organized religion or human beings alone. It encompasses all living things—animals, plants, trees—and extends even to what others might see as inanimate: rocks, water, thunder, and lightning. Everything has a spirit, a force, a wisdom, a life of its own. Nahganne, too, is part of this web of spirits. When our Elders describe Nahganne, they speak with the same respect they hold for the natural world.

The secrets our Elders carry about these giant creatures is closely tied to Indigenous ways of knowledge. While some will speak of Nahganne and share their knowledge, others remain silent. It is not out of fear but a sense of the sacred—a belief that some truths are not meant to be spoken lightly. This silence is both a strength and a challenge, for as our Elders pass on, so too do the stories and knowledge they hold. If we do not preserve these stories now, they risk being lost, forsaken by time.

I remember the lessons my grandmother taught me, and one of the most important was her warning: never hurt Nahganne. From her, I learned kindness—kindness to all living things. Hurting Nahganne is something our Elders would never allow to happen. In all my life, I have never heard of a Dene person harming them. Instead, our People show respect, even leaving offerings for Nahganne to take from our hunting and fishing camps. If Nahganne takes fish or meat, no one says anything bad about them. They must eat too, and there is much wisdom to learn from them—wisdom we have only just begun to uncover.

When I was a boy preparing for a hunting trip with my uncle, my granny gave me a serious look and said, "Be careful. Nahganne is out there." Parents always worried about their children in the bush, and for good reason. Out there, you gather water, wood, spruce boughs for the tent floor, and berries when the season allows. It's easy to wander off, but it's also dangerous—dangerous in ways we can't always see.

My family has had its own encounters with these creatures. My dad's sister, my auntie, was taken by one. It was autumn, and the family had set up a camp to fish for herring. Suddenly, a Nahganne appeared and grabbed my aunt. She screamed, "Ama, Ama!"—"Mother!"—and as her cries pierced the air, a great wind rose up. My auntie later said that Nahganne can control the elements, calling up the wind as easily as we gather wood. Hearing her cries, my grandpa took off after her, running hard until the Nahganne dropped her. Without hesitation, he scooped her up and carried her back to safety.

But her return came with a price. Among the Sahtu Dene, there is a belief: if a girl is taken by Nahganne and comes back, her life will be short. They say the fright, the terror of the experience, is too much for the heart. Just a week after my grandpa saved her, my auntie passed away.

I have been told that Nahganne's power goes beyond the wind. They can silence dogs and entire dog teams, bending their will. It seems to me that Nahganne are more concentrated in certain parts of the land—places where their presence feels strongest, where the air itself feels heavier, as though their unseen eyes are watching.

The second encounter with Nahganne that I know of happened in my hometown in the Northwest Territories during the 1940s. It involved the daughter of a widow who lived on the riverbank overlooking the Dehcho River. She was well known in our community, and, as a boy, I often helped her by chopping and splitting wood. The widow had only one child, a daughter, who had been trained by her husband as if she were a son. She learned all the skills Dene boys were taught to survive on the land—how to shoot, trap, fish, and set nets with ease.

Nahganne, as our Elders say, often roam near Dene camps, always searching for food. At night, the barking of dogs is our first warning. It might be wolves or bears, but many times, we suspect it's Nahganne. The dogs are our first line of defence, but even they are no match for Nahganne's strange powers. Despite all precautions, the widow's daughter was taken—just like my auntie. She had been alone, and as in so many stories of Nahganne, it happened in the autumn.

Later, the widow's daughter recounted her terrifying experience. She told my grandmother that Nahganne took her to the rocky summit of an old mountain. She remembered something being draped over her head, preventing her from seeing where she was being taken.

For two or three days, she was held there while the Nahganne went off to search for food. That's when she made her escape. But the Nahganne soon realized she was gone and followed her, screaming. She hid herself inside a hole in the ground, remaining perfectly still and quiet until morning. When the light came, she found her way back to her family, but the ordeal left her deeply shaken.

Like my auntie, the widow's daughter did not live long after her return. Among the Sahtu Dene, this is no surprise. It is said that when Nahganne takes someone, the fear they experience leaves a permanent scar on the heart, one that cannot be healed. The weight of what they endured is too great for them to carry.

Another story comes from another one of my relatives, originally from Great Bear Lake. She told me about a Dene man who worked at the Port Radium Mine in the 1940s—maybe even the 1930s—extracting ore, the same material later used to build the atomic bombs dropped on Hiroshima and Nagasaki.

At those mining camps, Nahganne were said to come around at night, moving near the family tents. The people inside could hear them communicating, their whistling cutting through the darkness and the rhythmic sound of stones knocking together. With a stone in each hand, one Nahganne would knock once, another twice, and then three times, as if signalling their presence to one another. The sounds were clear, deliberate, and unmistakable.

My own brother had a chilling encounter with Nahganne when he was just a boy. He and his best friend were on a boat on the Keele River when they spotted Nahganne standing on the land nearby. My brother told me he locked eyes with it from no more than 20 feet away. "You won't believe this," he told me. "His eyes were red." The memory stayed with him for years. When I asked him later, as a man in his forties, how he felt about it, his response was unforgettable: "When I think about it, it still haunts me to this day." I also spoke with the friend he was with, who confirmed the story. "We were just boys at the time," the friend said, "and it really shook us up."

Nahganne encounters seem to run through my family. I had another uncle, a skilled and experienced trapper, who once followed a trail of massive footprints in the snow. The tracks stretched far ahead, each stride too long to have been human. My uncle, convinced it was Nahganne, followed the trail for a long distance, eager to see where it led.

And then, the tracks stopped.

"There was nothing," he told me. "No sign of where it had gone. It was as if it turned into a bird and flew off."

This isn't the only time I've heard stories like this.

Other witnesses speak of the same thing—that Nahganne can shift its shape, perhaps becoming something else entirely or even slipping into another dimension. A recent account comes from an acquaintance up in Yukon who claims he saw something that defies explanation. He described watching a creature, which he identified as Nahganne, disappear right before his eyes. The creature, illuminated by the glow of a lamppost, lumbered slowly in his direction. As it approached, its form began to change—gradually becoming translucent, then transparent. The closer it got to him, the more its shape, density, and details seemed to dissolve, as if it were slipping out of this world. Then, as my acquaintance described it, "When it reached the lamppost, it was totally invisible—poof, gone. It was as if it had walked into a portal and vanished into another dimension." The encounter left him stunned, unable to explain what he had seen but certain of what he experienced.

Among the Dene, oral history is more than tradition—it is a living bridge connecting past and present. Our Elders speak of a time when our people were called the Rock People, as old as the rock formations themselves. These stories remind us that our existence is intertwined with all things and also tell of the first meeting of the animals, where laws were made to guide humans in their relationship with the land and its creatures.

One of my uncles shared a story like that with me that came from long ago about huge animals that used to live in the North. He told me that when the world was new, gigantic creatures roamed the Earth. Some were birds, others were four-legged beasts, but all were very dangerous. To escape these enormous animals, people would sometimes run out onto thin ice, luring the beasts to chase after them. The giant animals, heavy and unbalanced, would fall through the ice. At other times, my People would flee into the forest, where the massive creatures would get stuck between the trees, giving the People time to escape.

As the story goes, two twin brothers who had medicine power once built a huge trap to protect their village people from giant birds that had been threatening them. Using their supernatural abilities, the brothers piled a great mound of tree trunks on a lake. They melted the ice to create a trench and constructed a timber tunnel over the mound. By morning, two enormous birds flew over the lake and into the tunnel. The trap fell on them, just as the brothers had planned.

The giant birds had caused so much trouble that the brothers decided to eliminate them for good. The Elders encouraged their efforts, and the brothers used their medicine power to rid the land of the troublemaking birds. Once the fierce creatures were gone, the brothers foresaw that the era of giant animals would soon come to an end. True to their prediction, no one has ever heard of giant birds troubling my People since.

Among the Dene, especially our Elders, there are specialists in every part of the natural and spiritual world. Some carry the stories of the stars, others know the ways of animals, and still others hold the wisdom of plants. But when it comes to Nahganne, some will speak, while others remain silent, as if the knowledge is too sacred or unsettling to share. I often remind them, "We need you to pass this on to the younger generation. If you keep it to yourself, how will we honour our traditions and protect ourselves?"

Understanding Nahganne, then, is not just about unraveling mysteries or confronting fears. It is about reconnecting with wisdom that sees life in all things and respects the delicate balance the Creator has set for us. The Nahganne stories are not just tales of the strange—they are part of the sacred truths that guide how we live, how we respect the land, and how we honour the spirits that surround us. In sharing these stories, we honour not only Nahganne but also the spirit of the Dene, ensuring that this knowledge endures for generations to come.

That is why this story exists. It's not just to share what we know of Nahganne, the Sasquatch of the North, but to understand them—what they mean to our People and how to stay safe if we meet them in the bush. These are lessons and truths that have endured for generations, carried in whispers and shadows. Mahsi Cho.

"Shattered reflections
scatter the past, the void
awakens to
claim her at last."

7

THEATRE OF SACRIFICE

Maeve Wills

OTHERS SPEAK of marching to their sacrifice with devotion on their lips and glory in their hearts. For me, it's nothing like that. The so-called "honour" of it is nothing but punishment wrapped in ceremony. I'm 18. I should be chasing pleasure, uncovering life's possibilities. Instead, I'm strapped to a plank, shuttled through the streets of Athens, my ankles bound by cords that gleam like gold but bite like knives.

Each jolt sends waves of nausea rolling through me. Spectators line the passageway, their rhythmic cacophony rising like a verdict, hammering in my skull. What are they even cheering for? How can they watch me tied up like a lamb and call it noble? I've seen their faces before—laughing in the market, arguing over olives. Now they're gods, complicit in my fate. I try to make sense of their words, but they blur together, relentless and oppressive.

The cords bite into my skin with every jolt. My body aches, but it's the weight of their eyes that crushes me most: the spectators, their faces blurred yet unyielding.

This is what I get for being born here, now? My whole life? What was it for, just to end up like this?

A windblown Chorus rises above the din, grating against the air, each tone clashing like mismatched puzzle pieces. Every note, burrows under my skin. It's not just sound, it's a sharp, unrelenting force that claws at my bones.

Then I hear it. My name. Soft, distorted, impossible to ignore.

"Lenaea," a voice sings, low and reverent. It brushes against me like wind on glass, fragile and piercing.

Another voice follows, harsher, slicing through the first like a blade.

"Bearer of innocence. Do you see your purpose?"

I freeze, resisting the knowledge already etched in my fate. The chorus wraps around me, suffocating:

"The chosen walks the sacred path; the threads tighten with her steps."

A chill grips me as I strain against the bindings. Are they trying to terrify me? To prepare me? Or is this some prophecy I can't escape?

The plank beneath me jolts forward, carried by unseen hands. The passage opens into a grove cloaked in twilight. Ancient, gnarled trees stretch skyward, their branches, a canopy that chokes out the light. The air clings to me, thick with the scent of damp earth and metal—like blood soaked into the soil. Roots quiver as the chorus swells, carried on the wind.

"Do you feel it, Lenaea? The sacred path?"

The grove murmurs, the trees leaning in as though they're watching me. Tangled roots rise from the ground, draped in wilting garlands. Their cloying sweetness mingles with the sharp tang of decay. The chorus cuts through, sharp and clear:

"To die is to bind our mortality to the divine."

I pull at my restraints. "What do you mean?" My voice is hoarse, barely audible.

The answer comes, cold and unyielding:

"A thread pulls. It will not let you go."

The plank lurches forward, the roots shifting beneath me. My vision blurs, my thoughts pound against the deafening roar. Am I already dead? Or is this the first step into something worse?

The grove opens into a clearing, and blinding light forces my eyes to shut tight. I am still strapped to the plank, and when I open my eyes, I am at the centre of an amphitheatre's orchestra stage. This is no ordinary performance space. It's the heart of our Greek theatre, where the mortal and the divine converge.

Above me, thousands of spectators chant in unison. Their cries reverberate, but I do not comprehend. Their faces blur into a vast, collective force, binding me to the stage.

My gaze locks on the backdrop skene, its carved stone walls alive with images of sacrifice. My stomach lurches as I spot a familiar figure among them: a shadowed version of myself, a face frozen in terror. Is this a cruel coincidence, or am I staring at my own fate?

From the skene's yawning doorway, a black void that devours the torchlight, masked figures emerge, their movements deliberate, ritualistic. The satyrs follow, their goat-like legs striking sharp, rhythmic beats. Their masks, etched with savage ecstasy, seem alive, their bodies raw with untamed desire.

One satyr lingers in the shadows, his presence undeniable. When he steps into the light, the others retreat, their heads bowed.

He raises his arms, his voice cleaving through the stillness: "It is time. The play will unfold as it must. Step into the story Lanaea."

The crowd falls to a taut silence, the air thick with reverence and anticipation.

The satyr steps closer, his eyes fixed on mine, and speaks, his voice a deep, resonant murmur that pierces the quiet: "You tremble, and that is good. Fear tempers the fire within; resistance sharpens the edge of the soul."

My eyes stay fixed on him, unable to look away. "Who are you?" I ask, the question raw and unguarded, as though the answer might explain everything.

A faint smile curves his lips. "What am I? A guide. A test. The fire you fear and the escape you crave." He steps closer, his presence overwhelming. "Tonight, Lenaea, I am yours."

The spectators' excitement explodes, crashing over the amphitheatre like a wave.

My eyes dart back to the skene. The etched figures seem to breathe, eyes following my every move, shifting into a story I can't tear myself from: a girl carried into a grove, brought onto a stage, and consumed by darkness. The final image is clear—her soul is held aloft like a trophy.

The satyr gestures to the carvings. "This stage knows your story better than you do," he says, his smile widening.

The plank jolts beneath me, and suddenly I'm weightless, rising as though the stage itself has claimed me. The satyr stands below, smiling. His golden fur shimmers in the torchlight, his horns spiraling upward, casting shadows that dance across the stage. His piercing eyes gleam intelligence and hunger, his smile predatory and inviting.

His hand brushes my arm, and a wave of heat surges through my body. My essence pours outward, untethered and radiant. Around me, the actors and satyrs fall to their knees. The amphitheatre trembles as the Chorus emerges from the void, its chant rising like the rumble of the earth.

"The fire tests her trembling soul. The stage consumes to make it whole."

The satyr steps closer, his gaze locking with mine, voice softening, intimate, a secret echo: "I feel the fire coursing through you."

I tremble, my voice shaking ,and I gesture to the actors. "Why me? Why not them?"

"Because you resist, which makes the fire burn brighter. The actors bow as you rise. This stage belongs to you."

Energy surges through me, searing and intoxicating. It binds me to the stage, pulling me into the satyr's orbit. Together, we become a monument of light at centre stage, a vision of power and desire intertwined. The crowd gasps, their awe mingling with terror.

His voice vibrates in the monument of light, a tender whisper that coils in my mind. "Surrender to it, Lenaea. My fire can be your destiny."

The masked actors retreat to the edges of the stage, their movements muted as the monument of light trembles, flickering like a dying flame. Then, with a deafening crack, it collapses into a single, brilliant point of light.

The stage seems to hold its breath. For a moment, there is only darkness. Then the light explodes outward, illuminating the amphitheatre in a sudden burst of radiance. From its centre, we emerge.

The satyr steps forward first. He pauses, turning to extend a hand to me as though offering not salvation, but an irrevocable choice.

I step into the light, its heat searing through me, igniting every nerve. The air hums with a force beyond comprehension as I stand beside him, the weight of the amphitheatre's gaze pressing on my skin.

"Do you see it now?" he asks, his tone unyielding. "You and I are the fire. We are the story."

The crowd erupts in a thunderous roar, their cries rising and then falling into an awed, reverent silence, as if the amphitheatre itself is drawing breath.

My gaze darts to the skene. The structure's central orifce gapes open, the void pulsing faintly, its menace lingering in the shadows. At its centre, the girl, the shadow sister, reaches outward, her carved hand choreographing my steps with an unrelenting push. Her hollow eyes track me, full of accusation.

The satyr begins to speak to the crowd, an aside. His voice, low and deliberate.

"She stands there trembling," he murmurs, as though reflecting aloud. "Does she even understand what this stage demands of her?"

I stiffen, "What it demands of me? What do you mean?"

The satyr's head tilts slightly. "Fear sharpens your mind and quickens your soul."

The masked actors fall to their knees. The satyr's voice commands them. "Prove to me that she is the chosen one!"

The actors retrieve relics from the skene—fragments of scrolls, shattered mirrors, objects that thrum with power. Their movements blur into a frenzied ritual, their bodies flowing with a grace both primal and precise. Fragments of scrolls circle the actors; each bearing words I cannot read. The mirrors catch the torchlight, their cracks fracturing my reflection into something unrecognizable.

The satyr gestures to the relics. He holds one of the mirrors aloft, its cracked surface reflecting my face in jagged fragments.

"This," he says, his voice calm yet pointed, "is what you leave behind. The image of what you were."

He tosses the mirror to the ground. It shatters completely, the pieces scattering like stars across the stage. The actors fall prostrate as the Chorus rises again:

"Shattered reflections scatter the past, the void awakens to claim her at last."

An actor steps forward, offering a fragment of a scroll. The satyr holds it out to me, his smile sharp and expectant. My name is scrawled on its surface, half-burned, the edges curling.

"Will you read your fate?" he asks.

I reach for it. On it is written: "Chosen." But as I read the word, a question rises in my thoughts: Is this how I am supposed to feel? Power? Submission?

He says, "This is what the stage demands." His gaze glimpses the Shadow Sister. "But the choice is not yours alone."

He gestures to the spectators. "They watch, hungry for catharsis, their silence feeding the void. I am their voice, Lenaea. I speak what they will not say. I act what they dare not do."

The stage shifts, the skene's darkness receding as the satyr strides forward, his body radiant and glistening beneath the torchlight. I hesitate, but the power of instinct propels me forward. My legs wrap around his powerful torso as I climb onto his back. His fur is warm, dense, and alive with movement. It's wrong, it has to be wrong, yet I can't stop. Is it the ritual binding me, or is it him?

Each of his steps vibrates through me, his rhythm syncing with my heartbeat—a primal drumbeat that binds us together. The amphitheatre fades into shadow, the performance narrowing until it centres solely on this connection, this moment between us.

As we move, the stage becomes an extension of our performance, the boundaries of reality dissolving. His body beneath me is alive, deliberate yet wild, each movement charged with purpose. My thoughts churn, sharp and insistent. How much of him do I truly command, and how much of me is already his?

The question escapes my lips, my voice low but fervent. "How do I make you mine? Not just your body, but your mind and soul. How do I bind you to me?"

His body tenses beneath me, as though he hears the question as I am forming it. His reply is soft, measured, and unyielding. "You cannot claim me as a prize. To have me, Lenaea, is to give yourself. Entirely."

The play unfolds around us, actors moving like whispers at the edges of my awareness. Yet we remain its centre: a story within a story. For now, the presence of my Shadow Sister hovers in the periphery, her resentment eclipsed by the satyr's consuming presence.

The satyr kneels, his power no longer binding me, leaving only the raw connection between us, a connection as old as the theatre itself.

From the skene, the Chorus emerges, their movements deliberate, their robes shimmering with the hues of dawn and dusk. Their masks embodying the eternal duality of the theatre. Their chant begins, discordant at first, then rising into a haunting harmony:

"Lenaea, your love has transcended mortal binds. Yet the rite remains unfinished."

I rise, unsteady, my legs trembling as the Chorus forms a semicircle around me. Their voices intertwine, weaving a single, haunting refrain:

"The veil awaits, the threshold of transformation. Bring the essence of your journey towards its final form."

The satyr rises beside me, his voice low and charged with emotion. "The veil is ours to cross together, Lenaea. But it is your gift to lead."

I step forward, the faint glow of the threshold stretching out before me. My legs falter, not from exhaustion but from the weight of the choice before me. Each step feels like stepping into a story I may not survive to tell.

The amphitheatre blurs, its walls dissolving into translucent waves of memory. Yet even here, my Shadow Sister's form flickers at the edge of the skene, resisting the pull of light.

The Chorus swells into a crescendo:

"She walks the veil, the thread of fate unspooling. Her love shapes the cosmos; her soul binds the eternal stage."

The satyr follows, his steps in perfect harmony with mine. As we cross the threshold, the amphitheatre transforms into an expanse of endless light and colour. I feel my mortal body lift away, escaping to something lighter, freer, a form that reflects the union of my essence with his.

But even in this glowing realm, a shadow appears at the edges of the light—my Shadow Sister, no longer faint. Her hollow eyes devour the radiance, her movements mirroring mine as though she is a tether pulling me back.

The Chorus narrates, their tone solemn and absolute:

"She steps beyond the mortal frame, her love a beacon across the eons. Not death, but unity. Not sacrifice, but transcendence."

The satyr turns to me, extending his hand. His eyes, warm yet flickering with caution, shift briefly toward the Shadow. "You are no longer bound, Lenaea. We are equals now, and this stage is ours to shape together. You see only the sacrifice, but the stage is more than death. It is creation."

The amphitheatre dissolves into shimmering starlight, the satyr and I moving together, untethered from mortal constraints. For the first time, I feel whole—body, soul, and desire entwined. But even as the cosmos hums with echoes of our union, a question lingers, sharp and persistent: Is this wholeness real? Or another illusion, another act in the eternal play?

A faint vibration courses through me, familiar and inescapable as my Shadow Sister steps toward the starlight, her hollow eyes glinting. "You feel it, don't you?" she asks, her voice low and piercing. "The thread is pulling you back. It will not let you go."

I shake my head, the words trembling from my lips. "I crossed the threshold. I was free!"

She tilts her head, a smirk curling at the edges of her mouth. "Free? Or was it all a ceremony of illusion? You cannot escape me. I am every story you leave untold."

The starlight fractures, splintering into shards as my Shadow Sister reaches out. The satyr's voice cuts through the chaos, steady and commanding.

"Do not listen to her, Lenaea. She thrives on doubt."

But her voice grows louder as she turns to me. "Without me, you are incomplete. Without me, you are hollow."

The shattered starlight reforms, folding back into the amphitheatre, now silent and empty. The crowd, although complicit, bears no further witness. Only the satyr, my Shadow Sister, and I remain. The skene looms behind us, its façade carved with my story, its central orifice gaping wide, the void within swirling and alive.

The satyr tenses, his powerful frame rigid as he speaks, his voice heavy with sorrow. "I tried to save you but the stage must always have a story. And a player must always find... release."

My Shadow Sister steps into the light, her voice coaxing. "You cannot run from me," she says. "You created me. Now, you must finish what you began."

I turn to the satyr, my voice breaking with desperation. "Is this what jealousy demands—a life erased, a soul devoured? How do I stop her?"

The satyr's eyes soften, but his voice is grim. "You cannot stop her. This is the cost of your journey."

The Shadow Sister's smile widens as the void surges forward, its darkness spilling from the orifice like an unstoppable tide. The skene groans to life, its carvings shifting and rippling as if alive, the void reaching for me with an inhuman hunger.

"The void ... awaits," my Shadow Sister whispers, her tone soft and inexorable. "Surrender."

The void growls, its voice resonant and cold.

"You cannot fight a shadow that wears your face."

A final whisper escapes my lips, my breath shallow and fleeting: "If you take me, will anyone ever know I was here? Will even my memories disappear? "

The void pulsates now, its growl deepens, reverberating through the amphitheatre, shaking the very stones beneath my feet. I try to look away, but its pull is unrelenting, its hunger palpable. The void's reply is low, almost mocking.

"What is worse? Forever silence or forever screaming?"

Despair surges through me, and the void pulls me through the orifice into its eternal shadows. I am alone. The amphitheatre shakes, the ground beneath it trembling as the Chorus rises, their chant forecasting my doom.

Its hunger endless, the void awaits,
Mortality to divine it seals your fate.
Shadow Sister watches, sharp and grim,
For the next sacrifice to begin."

"I take the gravel turnoff past
a dilapidated road sign marker
half buried in sand
and weathered
to near nothing."

8

RISING SUN

Alex Soop

I AM JUST about to get on my phone and grill my brother when he unexpectedly calls at the very moment my fingers grasp the screaming smartphone resting in my cup holder. I shudder as my mind is lost in a roll of angered thoughts.

"Speak of the fuckin' devil," I say under my breath. I hit the answer button on my flashing phone. "Yo, dude," then, without waiting for him to answer, "Your buddy lied to me man. That son of a bitch, he—"

"Hey man, what's up?" answers my brother's buddy Darrel, unmoved it seems, by the string of cuss words I had directed against him. I'm briefly caught off guard by Darrel's unexpected call from my brother's phone, but ultimately, Darrel is the guy I need to talk to anyway.

"Hey," I reply in a calm, slightly sheepish manner. "I uhh—I think I'm lost, dude."

"Did you bring an old map like I told you? Like old, old?" he asks, his voice coming out all aged and crackly like we are corresponding through old World War II style comms radios. "I'm talking, like, 1970s to the early '80s old, man. The kind of stuff before personal computers and Google maps were even dreamed of—"

"Yeah, I managed to get my hands on an old map. But what's that gonna do, though? I've got a state-of-the-art GPS installed in my car."

"That won't do, man. Not at all," Darrel asserts. "This place is old, like, the government not putting it in their electronic database anymore old. And I'm pretty sure there's other reasonings behind it too. So, what I want you to do is pull over right now, break out the old map and pinpoint that part of New Mexico, exactly where you should be right about now. Call us back when you do it, cool?"

I'm skeptical but I sigh and say, "Okay, fine. Call you back in a minute or so." I tap the hang up button and flicker my headlights to make sure they're still on the bright beams. They are indeed, but the illumination only spreads through the flat and endless desert terrain like I was holding a cheap flashlight while riding a bicycle in the prairie flats at night. After a few miles of wasteland cruising, I am able to safely take a sharp right into a small roadside turnout. I pick up the old map, water-stained and musty from years of neglect, and identify my exact location, remembering the last destination my trusty GPS read to me.

I find it. The old road is nothing but an old squiggly line next to the main road markers.

I glance up and take in the desert dust, still lingering like frail ghosts. The dust enshrouds my headlight illumination like a gas attack as I scroll through my recent cellphone calls. Darrel finally picks up after four rings. "Yo," he says in a way that further irritates my shabby mood.

"Okay, gimme the details," I demand.

The line goes dead silent like he has hung up on me, until I hear the crunchy rattling of stiff papers. "Okay, I found it," he says, his breath ragged like he is just as excited as me. "What's your location right now?"

"I am on the 380 about halfway between the towns of San Antonio and Bingham. I—"

"Perfect. Look for an old sign marker that says, 'Rising Sun Hotel.' It'll be the only one standing in the area by a longshot. Once you come across it, take a turn going northbound. You'll travel about ten miles through almost nothing but plain old desert, and then you'll see it. Right there, and boom, you're there. Won't be hard to miss, man. If you get lost, just call us back. Hope you see her." He hangs up before I can either thank him or scold him.

My destination in mind is just where Buddy said it would be. I take the only gravel turnoff past a dilapidated road sign marker half buried in sand and weathered to near nothing. It reads, 'Rising Sun Hotel,' in old, non-reflective letters that are nearly falling off the antique sign. The bumpy drive runs through an ancient road filled with potholes and small debris from years of desert windstorms and neglect. At last, I see it looming beyond the range of my headlights—a tall, neon sign brightly lit, its radiance spraying over a small hamlet of buildings. I pull into the gas bar and general store first. No dice.

Must close early, I say to myself, slowing my speed as I coast past the gas pumps that look like they haven't been used in years, crimson rust draped over the metal like a person with a bad skin disease.

The hotel is the next building over. Three-tiered with something like minarets on the roof. Some of the chamber doors line the outer perimeter like an old-style jailhouse.

At least I'm not the only patron at this old hotel that lies smack in the middle of nowhere. There are four more vehicles: an SUV, a jacked-up pickup, and two older model sports cars that still look as though they're able to do damage in a street race. Beyond the fourth vehicle is an arrangement of about 20 motorcycles lined up in perfect order.

A darkened area of the lot is a more suitable place to park, out of the limelight and therefore less susceptible to being broken into. Bikers usually mean crime sprees. I pull in behind a dumpster, endowed with the same bouquet of rust.

I shut off my engine and wait, taking a second to gather myself before entering this strange property. By the sounds of the lively music pouring out from the open windows of the hotel's attached bar, there are plenty more patrons inside than the four cars and motorcycles declare.

I skip the bar's rough-looking, bouncer-free entrance and head inside through the motel's lobby entrance doors. Couldn't be more of an eerie omen, I think to myself as "Hotel California" plays through an old radio located in the waiting area.

"Good evening, sir," says a polite gentleman standing behind the reception desk, his eyes scanning a fat 1990's computer monitor. "Late night, isn't it?" A British accent. Way out here in the middle of the American wasteland.

"Uhh, yeah. It is. But I'm supposed to be meeting someone here."

The well-mannered counter clerk lifts his regard from the old-fashioned screen the size of an old tube television, and eyes me carefully. "I assume that you're not from around here. Am I quite right about that?" he asks in a cheery way.

"You can tell?"

"Well actually, nobody who steps through those doors is from around here. But hey, that's why I found it all the better to open this motel. Looking to check into a room for the night?" he asks, as he steps away from the computer screen and waddles alongside his side of the desk, organizing scattered papers and shooing away dust build up with his baggy blazer sleeve.

I don't have to think for a moment. Even after meeting up with my special someone, I wasn't planning on driving the four-hour journey all the way back home in the middle of the night. “Yes, please.”

The motel owner takes up position back behind the computer and waits patiently for me to approach. I rummage through my jeans’ back pocket and pull out my wallet. “How much for one night?”

“Fifty-two dollars exactly,” he says.

“Wow. Cheap.”

“The cheapest,” he asserts, winking at me. “I opened up this place with strong intentions of keeping the weary traveller happy.”

And that I am, with this price.

“And indeed, you have,” I say.

“As well, sir, if you are not tired just yet, you are more than welcome to treat yourself to a nightcap in the open-late, ye olde saloon,” says the clerk as he hands me the keys, his devilish smile not waning once throughout our brief engagement.

The guestroom locks are old fashioned. A key is the only way into my room rather than the modern, magnetized card reader. I shove the heavy door open with the tip of my shoes, and I am slammed with the reek of ripened mustiness and stout chlorine bleach. When I hit the lights, I see that the appearance of the room is much better than the smell of the place. A fairly comfy-looking, queen-sized bed lies in the centre of a beige carpet. The walls are covered in a 1970’s-era floral design wallpaper, a tangle of green vines overlapping fancy flowers. Two faux plants rest in corners of the room and the classic touch-tone phone, tube television, and pull-cord lamplight complete the decor. A small, two-tiered nightstand is posted by the bedside, an old Holy Bible resting in place.

The plan is to meet Annalise in the bar at exactly a minute past midnight. I settle into my room and shower. Shortly before midnight and all freshened up, I make my way downstairs and follow the sounds of the drifting music, along with the spicy aromas of southwest cuisine.

The saloon is lively but not packed. Garth Brooks is playing on the jukebox as a pair of couples two-step on the dance floor, the men in cowboy hats and women in striped button-up blouses. A few round tables are hosting patrons, each one deep in drunken conversation. I step to the bar, lit up by only two neon lights, one in the middle of the bar top and one near the ceiling, atop the mirrors edge.

"What'll you be havin'?" asks the barkeep as he struts toward me.

"A beer if you have—"

"—MGD? You look like a cold-filtered kinda guy," he says brightly, his voice carrying a distinct Southern inflection.

I smile and nod at him, feeling somewhat impressed by his capability to read his customers. But I guess that should be a given. "Yes, please."

He lifts open an old-fashioned cooler and snatches out an ice-cold Miller Draft, hand-cracks it and hands it to me. "First one's on the house, my friend. Management guidelines." He tosses his hand towel over his shoulder and leans in, almost whispering. "Waitin' on someone, are we?"

I knock back a refreshing shot, letting the suds trickle down my desert-dry throat. "Yeah," I breathe out. "She's supposed to meet me here,"—I glance at the wall-mounted clock— "in about five minutes, or so."

"Oooh la la, a special lady, huh?" he says friskily. "Well, she oughta be here soon then. It ain't too often I see a man stood up in my bar. Good luck brother." He nods at me with a mischievous smile and disappears behind a makeshift curtain leading to an off-limits back room.

She was late. Either that or she had decided to stand me up. I waited until a quarter past the stroke of midnight, nursing my one beer while I waited impatiently.

Now past 12:45 a.m., I am six beers, two shots of whiskey and one tequila deep into the night. My buzz is helping defuse the feelings of resentment and abandonment, but we all know that numbing sensation never lasts long.

"Hey, darlin," says one of the saloon's few remaining patrons. A pretty woman in her early thirties with skin-tight jeans and a halter top revealing a silvery piercing in her navel. Her chiselled body looks as though it was constructed in a laboratory. Her blonde hair is twisted into locks, the old style of the nineties; maybe even the eighties. Nothing too peculiar as I am sitting inside an even-more unusual bar. "She stood you up, didn't she?"

"Could be," I hiss in a low baritone, keeping my eyes forward and polishing off the rest of my beer in frustration. "It isn't like her though." I say. "Not like her at all. She's never done this. Ever."

"Well, it's like that now, darlin," she says pitilessly, one of her frisky hands landing on my forearm as she chomps on bubble gum in an enticing, yet annoying manner.

I ignore her attempt to seduce me, eyeing my wristwatch. "Well, it's getting late. I should probably turn in. It's a long drive back to where I'm from." I face the bar's expansive mirror, an assortment of half-gone spirits lining the shelving, and wave at the bartender. "Goodnight there, barkeep," I say, standing up and heading for the exit. "Thanks for the cut-rate drinks. I really appreciate it."

"You betcha, my friend. Real sorry she didn't show," he says as he slings the same hand towel over his shoulder and begins stowing away bottles of spirits. I nod politely and vacate the drinking chamber as fast as possible before the loitering seductress has a chance to give it another go.

The television programming is just as lacklustre as the screen it's being broadcast on. Dull colours flicker, with occasional blips of static interrupting as I drunkenly goggle an old sitcom on low volume, the background laughter sounding like echoes of water splashing against a wall. As infomercials take over and my eyelids finally begin to feel heavy, I hear knocks sounding like birds pecking at the door. I am jerked to consciousness, and a jolt runs through my body, putting my nerves on edge.

Adrenaline spike.

I had already settled my mind on the fact that Annalise wasn't coming. Any visitor, especially at 2:00 a.m., is entirely unexpected.

"That stupid seductress found my room, dammit," I whisper harshly, rolling off the bed and onto my feet. I creep to the door and peek through the dirt-smeared peephole. There stands Annalise. She stands impatiently, her head of lavish hair swinging from side to side like she is looking for someone who may have been shadowing her.

With excited, fumbling hands, I unlock the chain and deadbolt, and yank the sturdy door open. "Come in, come in," I tell her, grasping my beloved girlfriend's hand, and tugging her safely inside my cheap hotel room.

Annalise regards me with a tantalizing stare—the very gaze that I had fallen in love with over three years ago. "Hey," she says ever so sweetly, like a bird chirping for its first time, a delicate smile gracing her rosy lips.

No more hesitation, my arms fling around her as I squeeze tightly. "Oh god, I've missed you so much."

She breathes into my shoulder, her breath like cool ice. "Me too. Oh my god, like so much, you'll never know, baby." Our quiet, heartfelt embrace lasts a few more seconds. I wish it could last forever. She breathes out a complaining exhale and whispers, "I love you." And the last words like a dagger pierce to my heart. "I can't stay long."

I push out the dagger. "I love you too," I affirm, tilting my head back until I'm once again gazing into her tender brown eyes. Without saying more, I seize her hand and lead her out of the cramped coatroom foyer, guiding her further into the compact room. I sweep aside my jacket and small overnight bag from the bed, and we settle down, allowing seconds to stretch into minutes as we engage in a soul-reaching gaze, locking eyes.

It feels like an eternity since I last had the chance to lose myself in our love for each other, those eyes of hers resembling sweet, caramel-brown candies, decorated with lush eyelashes.

It isn't long before the stares turn to touches. And the touches turn to all-out caressing and kisses to each other's naked bodies.

I was always told that 3 a.m. is the witching hour. For the past few nights, I had awoken to the dreary still of the night, the dim red illumination of my alarm clock pulsing to the shadows of the darkness. This night is different of course. I rouse, feeling somewhat rested and truly relaxed, my arms snuggly strung around Annalise as she sleeps peacefully.

There is someone—or something else—in the room with us. A silhouette is standing tall and upright against the closed blinds, the perky red and green luminosity of the outdated neon sign pulsating at its back.

For heart-thrashing minutes I lie on my side, my peripherals trained on the statue-still intruder. All I see is arms at its side, no twitching of a finger. No weapons, perhaps. Finally, the adrenaline and dreadful delay are too much. I loosen my hold around my beloved and spring myself off the bed, fists clenched and at the ready.

"Alright mother—"

Emptiness.

Where the shadow of a person once stood has now transformed into emptiness, the only silhouettes being the crossbar outlines draped across the carpet, caused by the neon lighting beyond the window blinds.

A faint rustling of bed sheets and a creaking of the mattress, is followed by, "What are you doing, babe?"

Muscles still tensed up, I shift to face Annalise, her exquisite features with their almond-eyed allure illuminated by the alternating hues of red and green dancing across her face. As our eyes meet, her awakened charm eases my surge of anxiety. "I just—I thought I heard someone. You know how it is with these spooky, old-timey motels?"

She chirps out an apprehensive giggle and pats the empty space next to her. "Come. I'm so tired. I need you to keep me warm."

Before taking back to the bed, I take another glance around the room. Then peek out the blinds. The lot outside is as empty as a graveyard—or abandoned motel. Not wanting to alarm my love, I pluck together my threads of courage and join her. She wasn't lying. Her body is cold, like we were asleep in an overly air-conditioned room. Yet, the cheap room is void of any such luxury. In no time I am fast asleep, her cold physique cooling down my sprinting heart.

The morning desert sun always hurts my eyes. This time, the burning red ball seems to be magnified, its searing heat burning through the walls and staying affixed inside the stuffy motel room. I open my eyes fully, thoughts of cool water streaming into my head. Rolling onto my side, I pat the empty spot next to me.

I am up and awake like a jolt of coffee. "Annalise?" I half scream, my voice echoing coldly off the enclosing walls.

Once again, she is gone, perhaps sneaking out in the middle of the night. The dagger has returned, driving into my heart.

Every vehicle is gone. My car is nestled behind the lone rusting dumpster. Before heading to my ride, I take a last look around the deserted hotel parking lot. Tumbleweeds roll across the sand-speckled lot, pushed by a westerly wind.

Eyes.

Devilish eyes. Staring at me unkindly from somewhere beyond the array of darkened windows lining the three-tiers facing the parking lot. The feeling is too much, enough so that my stomach begins to churn. I steal my gaze from the emptiness and dash for my car, getting in and starting it up. I am out of the parking lot in a haste, flooring past the vacant general store with a cloud of billowing dust in my wake.

Speeding down the sandy, two-lane road, my eyes are still glued to the rear-view mirror, my heart slowing in pace for every retreating foot I am away from the creepy motel.

DING!

I jump at the sudden outcry of my smartphone, my white-knuckled grip on the steering wheel coming loose as I nearly swerve into the sandy shoulder of the narrow gravel highway.

"Holy shit!" I scream, loud enough that my voice hurts my own ears. I take a glance at my phone nestled in my cup holder. Clive. My eccentric little brother texting to see how I'm doing. Perhaps to see if I'm still alive.

The speed I am travelling would be more than enough to get me pulled over, but I keep on until I see the looming, fragmented sign with the hotel's name scrawled across it in broken lettering. I barely slow down, letting my low-profile tires pay the price as I screech onto the main highway.

Now's the time to slow my speed. I take the first roadside turnout, letting my overworked car coast to a halt, the reek of burnt rubber still evident. I opt to call my brother rather than to text him of my good news.

"Hey," Clive answers after two rings. "Well? Did you see her?" His husky, teenage voice is painted in an overabundance of enthusiasm.

"I did," I answer nonchalantly.

"Awesome. So, you on your way back now?"

"I am."

"Cool. Will you be back in time for the wake?"

"I should be. If I drive a little over the limit."

A pause. Followed by my brother's voice turning low and empathetic. "I'm really glad you got to see her one last time before we bury her and she crosses over through the gates of Heaven."

"Me too, little brother. Me too." I hang up and casually pull back onto the highway, punching the accelerator until my car is freewheeling just past the posted speed limit.

"Something made my
skin crawl, like the sensation
of being brushed by
spider legs in the dark."

."

9

THREADS IN THE SHADOWS

Laurier Tiernan

SWIRLING in the mists of a tight-lipped town a short walk from the Sea of Japan, myths are whispered in hushed tones. The caution surrounding them feels like the fear of rousing a sleeping dragon... or perhaps something smaller, something that crawls and spins its web in quiet corners.

These tales began with the birth of Grandmother Kimiko and her five sisters. Entering the world in the early 1910s, each of them possessed an astonishing intellect. Cackling as a hexad, they hovered like a coven, their laughter unsettling. By old age, no one dared cross their paths. The townspeople knew the sextet harboured powers they barely dared to acknowledge, whispering of unseen forces that swirled around them, weaving intricate, invisible threads.

Kimiko had not been destined for a life of wonder, or so the elders thought. She was meant to marry, bear children, and labour in the shadow of her husband, like the other women in the village. But Kimiko's mind was guided by odd forces from beyond the veil, and her calligraphy and needlecraft were said to hold something more than just skill. They seemed to trap secrets within their fine, delicate lines.

She surrounded herself with books, their cloth-bound volumes piled high like silent sentinels on groaning shelves and around her bed. It was said that if you stepped too close to these volumes, you might feel a soft tickle, as though the air itself held the faintest trace of silk threads, brushing against your skin before vanishing. The villagers who felt it never stayed long.

Not far from Kimiko and her sisters, a boy named Ichiro was born into a life of poverty. Ichiro moved through life always wary, always restless. His heart was hardened by the bitterness of his struggles, and when it came time to wed, it wasn't for love but for what Kimiko's family could offer—a way out, a path to something more. Little did he know that by stepping into her life, he was caught in the web of her strange and secret world.

While Ichiro was away at war in Manchuria, their only child, Isamu, was born. Isamu grew up shy and quiet, with a gentle smile that masked something peculiar behind his eyes, something that made people uneasy, like the feeling of being watched in an empty room. He excelled in his studies, much like his father, but there was a weight to him, a sense that his life was connected to something older, something hidden beneath the surface of the everyday world.

When Isamu met Keiko, a dancer whose bloodlines flowed from the Samurai class, it was as though their fates were tied from the start. Their love story grew into a village legend, but beneath the surface, dark currents flowed. Keiko's grace was mesmerizing, but those who watched her too closely sometimes claimed to see strange shapes in the shadows as she moved—fleeting, like the glint of spider silk.

Their daughter, Emi, combined her father's sharp intellect with her mother's beauty. Suitors flocked to her, but she swatted them away like flies. Her strength was undeniable, but there was always a quiet tension between her and the world around her, as if she, too, was caught in a web of unseen threads, pulling her in directions she didn't always understand.

Years later, I would enter this strange mix. Born on the frozen Canadian prairies, I had always felt out of place, haunted by visions and an inexplicable connection to the otherworldly. When I met Emi, it felt like fate. We were married quickly, and despite the mysteries she kept from me, it became clear that she shared the same gifts that had followed her family for generations—the same ability to sense things others couldn't see.

Emi's grandmother Kimiko had a milestone approaching that year. In just a few months, she would turn one hundred. She had long outlived Ichiro, who had become an alcoholic and beaten her more times than she cared to remember. Every year that she survived felt like a triumph, and she took joy in spending time devouring her books and newspapers, as if the printed page was cheering her on to immortality. Weeks shy of her hundredth birthday, something shifted. She fell ill, asking for a doctor—a request that was unlike her. Within days, her tiny lungs ceased their rhythm, and her fierce spirit slipped away.

Emi and I were summoned for the funeral and to sort through Kimiko's belongings. She had occupied a room in Emi's parents' house for fifty years, fiercely guarding her solitude. As we crossed the threshold, the air felt thick, heavy with dust and time, but also with something else. Something that made my skin crawl, like the sensation of being brushed by spider legs in the dark. No one had entered her space in a long, long while; she kept it entirely to herself, rarely discarding a thing. The room was frozen in time: a lonely single bed pressed against the left wall, with a towering armoire looming behind its headboard. The room felt suffocating, as though the very space was woven tight with her past. Every time I stepped too close to the corners, I couldn't shake the feeling of being watched, of something small and quick darting just beyond the edge of my vision.

For the next five days, we worked steadily, hauling trash and recyclables, our efforts ultimately yielding truckloads of discarded belongings. Yet amid the dust, clutter and much to my astonishment, I received gifts which would never leave me. On the first day, as I swept a cleared section of the floor, I glanced at Emi. "Grandma says she hid some money in her dresser," I murmured, seemingly out of the blue. Sure enough, Emi discovered sacks of coins, many of them antiquated. It felt too coincidental, too guided, and though I tried to laugh it off, I couldn't shake the feeling that something was leading us through the room, weaving us through its secrets.

As Emi continued to empty the dresser, she sighed, realizing much of Kimiko's clothing would have to be burned, steeped in the unmistakable scent of medication, the musty residue of time. "Old people's smell," Emi whispered, wrinkling her nose, before gesturing for me to join her at the door for yet another trip to the dump. It felt as if with every load we carried out another shadow lifted, revealing pieces of her spirit Kimiko had left behind for us to discover.

The second day of reclaiming Grandmother's room felt lighter. Breakfasting on rice, fish, and miso soup, as well as fresh pears for dessert, we could see more space on the bamboo flooring emerge from beneath the clutter. Sunlight flooded through the dusty air, illuminating corners that hadn't seen light in years.

Still, though, I felt Grandmother Kimiko tugging at me. *Look in the walls!* her voice echoed. I laughed, a bit annoyed and in my own mind, without speaking a word, asked, *There's nothing in the walls really, is there!* I scanned around for any evidence that she might be guiding me. The air shifted lighter for a moment, but it only deepened my unease. It felt as though we were disturbing something, tugging at threads that had been left to rest for far too long. Every glance at those dark corners made me think of spiders—quiet, patient, always watching from the depths of darkness.

Jarring me out of a dream, Emi sighed in exasperation, "Can you help me move this wardrobe? Dad wants us to break it up and burn the wood in the back yard." Then, to our astonishment, as we pried it from its home of half a century, the wall behind the wardrobe opened up into a bookshelf; lined with dusty cloth-bound volumes, and antique glassware. *Look in the walls,* Emi's grandma had pleaded, and here it was, a secret unearthed, waiting to be discovered.

The third day after Kimiko's passing was steeped in silence. Not a whisper from her spirit reached my ears, and despite my clairaudience, I began to wonder if I had imagined the faint echoes of her presence. We continued our labour, hauling stacks of yellowed newspapers from beneath Kimiko's bed and ferrying them off to be recycled.

On the morning of the fourth day, Emi and I surveyed Kimiko's room with a sense of deep satisfaction. Most of the bamboo flooring was visible now, and we marvelled at how well the vintage mats had endured the passage of time. The hidden bookshelf, now cleaned and organized, lent the room a touch of unexpected elegance. In the corner, the small altar felt like a sanctuary, radiating a sense of peace.

Then, just as we were absorbing the room's transformation, I felt it again—Kimiko's voice, faint but clear. *Check inside the ceiling.* The hairs on my neck stood on end. I glanced at Emi, who seemed not to have heard anything, her gaze fixed on the altar. I took a deep breath, wondering what secrets lay hidden above, waiting patiently for someone to find them.

Grandma Kimiko, there's nothing... inside... that ceiling, I thought, wondering if I had finally lost my marbles. But my musings were cut short as Emi called out to me, "Could you vacuum the closet, please?" I felt my heart skip a beat. "Yeah, sure," I replied, not fully processing her request. As I stepped into the closet, poking my head past the doors for the first time, I felt an inexplicable pull to look up. And there it was. A trap door, hidden in the ceiling.

"No... way," I muttered, failing to stifle a chuckle.

"What's so funny?" Emi asked, a curious tilt to her voice.

"A trap door in the ceiling," I replied, staring at it in disbelief. "I'm going to check it out." "Your grandmother wants me to," I said, more amused than I expected to be.

"Check it out then," Emi said with a nervous laugh, her curiosity getting the better of her.

Armed with a flashlight, I carefully pushed open the trap door and hoisted myself up. As I climbed into the attic, the air grew colder, and a strange sensation prickled at the back of my neck. The small space was filled with forgotten briefcases, old books, and a thick layer of dust, but it wasn't what I saw that terrified me—it was what I felt.

The beam of my flashlight caught a thin, shimmering thread stretching across the rafters. My breath spasmed, and I felt an overwhelming sense of dread wash over me. I followed the thread with my eyes and realized it wasn't alone. There were hundreds of them, glinting in the darkness like delicate strands of silk. They seemed to pulse, almost alive, vibrating as if disturbed by something unseen.

Suddenly, a soft rustling echoed from the far corner of the attic. My heart pounded as I slowly turned the flashlight toward the sound. The beam of light revealed a mass of webs, thick and tangled, covering the entire corner. And then I saw it—something moved within the webs, shifting slowly. My breath caught in my throat as a shape emerged: a large, spindly figure with too many legs, its body glistening in the dim light.

It wasn't a spider. It was something else, something ancient and eerie, as if spun from the very fabric of Kimiko's secrets. Its eyes glowed faintly in the shadows, and its long, delicate legs moved in a way that was too smooth, too graceful to be a simple creature. It was watching me, patient, like the threads it spun were part of something far greater—an intricate web woven through time, binding Kimiko, her family, and now me.

I felt the pull of the threads tightening around me, as if they were guiding me deeper into the web, as though I was part of this ancient connection, something I had unknowingly walked into when I married Emi.

Panic surged through me, but just as quickly, something else followed—a strange calm. I thought of Kimiko, her life, her fierce independence, her desire to protect those she loved. This... thing... wasn't here to harm. It was here to watch, to ensure the threads remained unbroken, to see that the secrets Kimiko had carried for so long would not be lost.

I exhaled slowly, lowering the flashlight, and as I did, the creature receded into the shadows, the threads around me slackening. The attic felt less oppressive, as though it had been waiting for acknowledgment, for someone to understand the balance it held.

"There's nothing dangerous up there," I called down to Emi, my voice steady. "Just... old things. Things that belong here."

As I climbed back down, the weight on my chest lifted. The fear that had gripped me earlier faded, replaced by an understanding that the webs were part of Kimiko's legacy—threads of protection and connection, woven to ensure her family would always be watched over, even after she was gone.

On the fifth and final day, Emi's mother, Keiko, asked if Kimiko's spirit was at rest. I listened, trying to sense the presence that had been with us from the start, but for the first time, I felt nothing. The room was still, silent.

Keiko approached me with a thoughtful look. "Do you think Grandmother's spirit wants anything else before she rests?" she asked. I centred myself, listening for any lingering echoes of Kimiko's presence.

Maybe some white flowers on my grave, her voice came, faint but clear. I turned to Emiko. "Did Grandmother have a favourite colour for flowers?"

She paused, slightly taken aback. "Well, we usually put white flowers on people's graves," she replied, with a hint of wonder.

"Yes," I said, nodding. "That's exactly what she asked for."

We placed white flowers on Kimiko's grave, her favourite. The air felt lighter, and this time, I glanced back at the house with a different sense. The threads that had bound Kimiko's life, those delicate, invisible strands, were still there, but now, they felt like guardians. Waiting, but with kindness.

When Emi spoke of her grandmother's passing, she said, "She just up and left." But I knew better. Some webs are never truly abandoned. They simply shift, watching over those who remain.

"She never fully controlled when she entered dreamworld, yet the path was always clear when it was about to happen."

10

TOUGH LOVE

Lynda Partridge

ALIANA often felt that being a skinny young woman with short-cropped black hair made her invisible to the outside world. Since childhood, she had tried to crawl into her skin to avoid being seen and to avoid being touched. She couldn't understand why the other kids called her "Red Skin" when actually she was a hue of brown. So many homes, so many escapes. So much she still didn't understand. She had cut her long, silky black hair to be less visible but so far it didn't seem to help. The tattered oversized sweatshirt, weathered blue jeans, and scuffed short army boots did not achieve her desired goal of invisibility in the world either.

She asked herself, *How am I still alive after all that has happened to me, all the trauma?* She knew there were lessons to be learned but for the life of her she couldn't figure them out. Bouncing from couch to couch in different people's houses trying to get a handle on things wasn't helping. As had happened before, she wondered if this was the real world for her—or was the other place her actual life? It was very confusing.

She looked around the room she found herself in. It was the living room of a woman she had recently befriended—a nondescript woman whose name she'd already forgotten. *Oh yeah, that's right ... this new person in my life offered me this safe spot in her apartment so I can sort things out. Whoever she is, she must have gone out.*

Aliana sighed to herself, *at least I know I'm still in the human dimension. That's a start.* She gazed around a little fearfully, but sensed that no one was present, so she curled up as small as she could, sinking into the folds of the over-stuffed cushions on the couch. *Okay, I'm losing it for real this time. Gotta get outta here.* She still mumbled to herself about the discrepancies she couldn't understand. *What the heck!*

Aliana doubled herself into that familiar blanket of nothingness. Such a strange feeling each time, yet oddly comforting and familiar. She never fully controlled when she entered dreamworld, yet the path was always clear when it was about to happen. She felt comforted by the constant swoosh of warm air enveloping her. Sometimes she could hear what she felt was a soft, melodic sound, an oddly familiar, comforting one. This warm swoosh sound and feeling were always her introduction to switching dimensions.

She waited for the visual evidence to show she had crossed worlds. *What will I see this time when I open my eyes?* Each time she entered the dreamworld, it was a bit different than the last visit, but was always recognizable. She thought of those first visits as a young child, when she had questioned what was real and what was simply a filler spot in her head to escape the atrocities of her young life. As Aliana grew older she met trusted friends who visited the dreamworld and, fortunately, taught her more about it.

Her trusted friends had explained to her that it was not the spirit world, although some people confused it with that. Instead, it was another dimension to which not every-one was able to readily travel. It was similar to going into outer space—but without a spaceship or need for a space-suit. Aliana welcomed the comfort and familiarity this dreamworld dimension provided her.

What will you see this time when you open your eyes? Shake off the human world Aliana, and sink into our dream-world landscape.

The landscape in dreamworld changed according to her age and what was happening in the human world. When she was around five or six years old, she had been a little girl in the back of a covered wagon. Whenever she crossed over into dreamworld, she would be sitting in the back of the wagon travelling to some unknown destination. There were always two beings—a brother and sister sitting with her and the three of them would dangle their feet over the edge of the back end of the wagon. She was always surprised they seemed to know who she was, but she didn't know them. She always recognized their familiar smell and the design of beadwork on the hide clothing they wore. It was always the same outfit on each of them, unlike her own clothes, which were always whatever she was wearing in her real human world when she crossed into the dreamworld.

The scenery was also strangely familiar, yet unknown. The ride in the wagon was always smooth—but how could that have been possible in a wagon with wooden wheels, travelling on a dirt path? There were always mountains in the background that changed through different shades of purples and pinks and blues. The covered part of the wagon limited her view but staring out from behind the wagon, this is what greeted her eyes. Strangely, she had never seen any other beings, but as a child she never really made that connection. It had always brought a sense of comfort to her, something familiar and safe. It had originally been by accident that she would cross into dreamworld and it only happened when she fell asleep.

She learned at a young age to differentiate between when she was actually just dreaming and when she was crossing into the dreamworld dimension. Dreams were something most people experienced and weren't as vivid and concrete as the human world. The dreamworld dimension however was like walking through a door into another room. Nothing was distorted. You looked exactly as you did in the 'real' world. Of course, the environment was purposefully manipulated to look like things that were familiar to you or that meant something to you. After all, if you crossed disembodied into the air and space of dreamworld, there was a good chance you'd lose your mind. As she became accustomed to the transfer process, she learned to have more control over when it happened.

Each time she visited dreamworld, the two beings who met her would reveal a little more about it. She came to understand that in actuality, her body remained behind and that she became just spirit and soul in that dimension. The form she took was just so she didn't lose a grip on 'reality'. It was reassuring to have a body that could see and feel, as that is what she was used to in her human world. The dreamworld beings manifested in forms that she could relate to and not be afraid of—especially in her younger years. They also seemed to have a different method of tracking time. *I wonder who these beings really are? How do they see each other? Always the same or ever-shifting?*

She had always envisioned herself as having been kidnapped by aliens in her human world so she decided that in a way, a covered wagon was one way of being 'kidnapped'. No matter how you looked at it, the whole situation was still pretty freaking strange. Through the years, she wondered if, like in a movie she had once watched, she was actually lying in a hospital bed, restrained because she was nuts and in fact nothing was real. She had even grappled with the idea that she was dead and was just too stupid to realize it yet.

What she did learn to do was to hide this world from the other humans in the dimension where she spent most of her time. She knew that the dreamworld dimension was only accessible to a few people, and once she had discovered that, she had started to embrace it.

She found that she no longer had to 'fall' asleep, but that she could will herself into a sleep state while still being technically awake. It had taken years of practice but other than the time warp that happened on occasions like this time, it was a pretty seamless transfer. Aliana was hoping that by visiting dreamworld she could figure out how the time warp had happened and what she could do to correct it.

"Well, well, look who just couched her way in once again," Girl's voice said. "Aliana, shake off the human world. Focus on dreamworld."

"Hey, hey, Aliana, where have you been?" asked Boy. We thought maybe you had deserted us."

"Yeah, yeah, I know you've just been saving up all your tough love just for me," Aliana responded groggily and somewhat sarcastically. "Seems to me last time we connected, you said I was probably a lost cause, that I didn't get it. Your humour definitely escapes me. What do you call it… dreamworld humour? Give me a couple of minutes—"

She shook her head once again. It always took a few minutes to get 'grounded' as these beings liked to play little head games with her sometimes just to see if she is paying attention. I'm happy, she thought, that the covered wagon scenario ended a few years back. I never was able to wrap my head around why I would be abducted or kidnapped by 'cowboys.' Isn't it always the little white blonde-haired princess who is abducted into the savage Indian village? Why would a skinny black-haired Indian kid like me be abducted into the wagon train headed to parts unknown? Maybe this dreamworld will bring more resolve.

Whoa, whoa, politically incorrect thoughts once again. Yes, it was always the Indigenous abducting the non-Indigenous into their villages and adopting them as one of their own to replace someone who for one reason or another was gone.

So, how is the dreamworld going to look and feel this time? she wondered. The dreamworld set had been replaced many times over depending on what was happening in her life. The only constants had been Boy and Girl in every dreamworld experience. They manifested in different ways, but they were clearly always the same beings. Aliana often felt like she was switching movie sets each time she entered this world. It was a constantly moving target and sometimes the set would change while she was in it. If she became complacent about where she was, it was made abundantly clear to her just where she wasn't.

As she moved more fully into dreamworld, she said, "I can't do this anymore. I can't just keep jumping in and out of dimensions. I don't know why I can do this, and I don't know what's supposed to be happening when I do this. You keep telling me I don't belong in this world, yet every time I jump dimensions here you are. Like seriously, are you just spending your lives lurking by the door waiting for me to appear? Do you get some perverse joy in watching and listening to my scattered thoughts every time? It's been at least 15 plus years we've been doing this same dance, and yet you still won't tell me why or how. Are you really the spirit world playing head games with me?

Girl's voice answered first, "We're not dead Aliana! We keep telling you we are not spirits. Quit going to séances to try and reach us through your wacky humans. And what's with you asking the Creator to make us disappear as though we're not real. Here's a news bulletin for you. It's the same Creator in all dimensions. Yeah, that's right, I said all dimensions. You seriously thought your dimension and this one are the only ones?"

Boy's voice chimed in, "Think again, girly. Glad you're here but wake up a little. It's been a lifetime, albeit so far a short lifetime, but still you're cutting into our time here. It's time for you to get it. We've gently pushed you towards understanding but you're one thick stump, you are. Think about it. You went back into your human world and you lost a huge amount of time. You don't even know where your body is in that dimension. Oh, and for the record, you're not dead and you're not restrained in a bed in some mental hospital somewhere."

Aliana gasped. "How do you even know that?"

"Well, you don't think you're the only one who can jump dimensions do you? How very egotistical of you," said Girl. "You keep coming here to dreamworld looking for answers but think about it. What answers are you looking for? What answers have you been looking for all these years? Since you were five years old you've been mindful of the fact that you can travel here."

Boy's voice picked up the pace. "You always blame everything on everyone around you. Yes, there are things you can't control, but there are things that you can control. Why don't you concentrate on them instead of all the other stuff? Geeze, Aliana. It's frustrating to watch in our dimension so it must be frustrating for you in your dimension and for everyone watching and listening to you. Snap your thinking head on. You're not a kid anymore. We're not going to be gentle with you."

Aliana looked down at her feet and realized she was floating, and the two beings who had always looked like a brother and sister were morphing back and forth in a kaleidoscope of colour. No shape, just a fusion of colours. "What the hell. What are you two idiots doing? I'm going to vomit, if that's even possible here. Give me back a floor and plant my feet back on it. Quit using me for your personal entertainment. You've gone completely bonkers." And with that, the swirling colours abruptly stopped and Aliana collided with the floor.

The colours, however, kept changing shape. Always two: one male one female: a priest a nun, then a rabbi and a ballerina, then a horse and a dog, then a pig and a dragon wearing a skirt, then a giant woman and a tiny man, then a tiny woman and a giant man.

"Enough already," Aliana screamed. "You have my attention." Aliana shut her eyes and slowly opened them again. This time she was sitting in a living room on a couch identical to the room in the apartment where she had started her journey into the dreamworld dimension.

Across from her, sitting in two separate armchairs were the two beings, once again manifesting as the Boy and Girl shape she was accustomed to. "So here we are. Or are we? Or where are we? Are you dreaming, Aliana? Or are you in the dreamworld or are you in your human world?" they asked in unison, taunting her. "You do know we die in this dreamworld dimension as well, right? And just for the record, we'd like to see you figure out your demented lifestyle while we're still alive and breathing."

Aliana sighed and asked, "What happened to the nice comforting beings you were when I was a kid? You're more like devil apparitions now!" With that, they both transformed into cackling, clownish devils.

"Seriously, you both sound like witches." The pair of them just sat there with their eyes boring into hers while they altered slowly back into their human forms.

"We're messing with you," Boy laughed

Girl asked, "Why are you here, Aliana?"

"Because you keep pulling me into your world to amuse yourselves."

"Nice try and great idea, but no," Girl said. "Think about it. When is the first time you crossed over? What was happening in your life?"

Aliana thought about it for a few minutes. She saw in her head that very first visit. She had just fallen against the huge fish tank in the family rec room in the basement and smashed the glass to smithereens. What she remembered most vividly were the goldfish all flopping and gasping for air on the carpet and someone yelling her name screaming, "What have you done?" She remembered being whisked away into the back of the covered wagon and being talked to by these two sitting across from her and wondering what the hell was going on. The flopping fish, broken glass, and water-drenched carpet disappeared. The next thing she remembered was being in a bathtub and being told to calm down and stop being hysterical. That was her very first trip into the dreamworld dimension and it was the beginning of her questioning her sanity for many years to come.

"Yeah, yeah, I remember. It was the fish incident."

Girl and Boy smiled at each other. "And why and how did you get to us that very first time?"

"I fricking don't know. I thought I'd passed out and died."

"Think a little more."

"I suppose I wanted to disappear before I got in trouble for breaking the fish tank and those flopping dying fish were freaking me out even as a kid."

" And so...?"

"And so I disappeared, or at least I thought I did, into your world."

"Aha. And what about all the other times you've ended up here? What has made you want to cross over?"

"I suppose every time I wanted to disappear or couldn't deal with what was happening at the time."

"But remember when you crossed back that first time?" asked Boy. "You were somewhere different than where you were when you came into our dimension. You went from the floor, to our dimension, and returned to find yourself in the bathtub. You never did figure that one out did you?"

"So?"

"So you were dealing with the situation," said Boy.

"What? That doesn't make sense!"

"Aliana, whenever you come here it's always when you're in a stressful situation" Girl said. Boy nodded in agreement. "We never see you when you're in a joyful or happy situation."

"Who do you look to then, when you're happy?" asked Girl.

Aliana gave it some thought and realized she always gave thanks to the Creator when life was good. When she asked Creator for help she usually ended up in dreamworld.

"We've already told you we have the same Creator here," said Girl and Boy together.

"But you fix things for me when I come here," replied Aliana.

"No, we don't," said Girl.

"Yes, you do. I couldn't survive without this dimension."

"Yes, you can," Boy insisted.

"No. I can't. There's no prejudice and racism here."

"Well, duh! There's also no shapes or colours," said Girl. It's not Utopia here, Aliana. You only see what Creator allows you to see."

"I'm confused. These are two different worlds?"

"Are they? Or do you just think they are?" asked Boy.

"Stop it. I know I'm in the dreamworld dimension."

"Yes, you are," said Boy. "But remember you are in both worlds. This isn't an escape route. For some reason Creator gave you the gift of visiting us here. That doesn't happen for all humans."

"Think about it, Aliana. Why are you here?" asked Girl. What are you learning? What impact will this have in your human life? It's time for you to go back to your home and figure things out."

Aliana decided that this was the worst day of her life. She couldn't figure anything out. She was hopeless.

"Just give me hint, will you?" She closed her eyes and wished everything away. There was a warm swoosh of air, and she could hear concern in their voices as she left dreamworld dimension.

"Maybe it was too soon."

"Maybe we should have given her more time."

"What if she doesn't figure out Creator is with her everywhere?"

The warm swoosh of air enveloped her body and carried her away from dreamworld to awaken her groggily back in human reality. Reflecting on Boy and Girl's argument and their tough love for her allowed her to appreciate that the feeling of the dreamworld can be carried into the human world.

Aliana thinks, *I can feel the swooshing calm melodic sweet sound. This is overwhelming. Creator is with me. I don't need to travel to see Creator.* She looked around her. She saw she was still in her new friend's apartment—the new person in her life who had offered this safe spot so she could sort things out. So, there she was, still burrowed into the couch cushions.

Everything flows between the dimensions. The human world and the dreamworld are not independent of each other. Then, in a moment of insecurity, she thinks, *Wait, is that all I am supposed to learn?*

After a moment or two of grogginess, the realization came to her: *No matter which dimension I am in, I control nothing in it except myself. Boy and Girl have nothing to do with who I am; they are a manifestation of my trauma and they change all the time. I remain the same in both worlds. I am me. To cope, I can bridge the two worlds into one. I don't need to drift between two different worlds. I control me. I don't need to change worlds anymore. Boy, Girl, or trauma do not determine who I am; I do. I need to heal from the trauma and change me. I need nothing special. I just need to believe. I need to change too.*

Aliana was indeed still alive after all that had happened to her. She found that a way to cope with her trauma was to be visible to the world and to deal with things as they happened, one at a time. Tough love had paid off.

"Somehow, I can sense an energy like the static you feel in your fingertips when you touch cold metal."

11

A TRAIN RIDE IS A LIFETIME

Uchechukwu Umezurike

The Bird

A bird perches on the fence outside my kitchen window, round, like a tennis ball. Her back is the shade of green in the early days of autumn. Her belly is a sharp yellow. She has a black crown on her head, like a peaked cap. I want to open the window to look at her more closely, but that will scare her off. So, I don't. The bird watches me watching her.

I can imagine how beautiful she would look in photographs. But I don't have my phone on me right now—I haven't seen it for a while. I haven't called anyone lately. No one has bothered phoning me in the last few days, either. It feels liberating not to be disturbed by calls from relatives or friends. My wife can no longer complain about seeing me on my phone.

The dishes haven't been washed. I reach a hand into the sink, and the bird screeches at me. I am wondering what has caused her alarm when she lifts in midair and darts straight at me.

The image of shattered glass flashes before my eyes, and I jump back.

The bird thrusts her breast against the window.

Thump. Thump. Thump.

The bird starts scratching the pane with her talons, as though possessed by something uncanny. I lean over the sink. I tap the window, upsetting the bird even more. She screeches again, then flies away.

The Man

My car is not in the driveway. My wife's is not there, either. She and our son have left already. The front of our house is piling up with squelchy red leaves from the maple tree. I should rake, but not now. I head for the train station in Emmett Tille, a ten-minute walk from our house. I don't mind the morning walk. It is all blue sky, and sunny.

A clan of geese squawks above me. I refuse to think about that crazy bird that tried to spoil my day. I only started taking the train recently because I used to be unable to bear the assault of body odours and fragrances, but they no longer churn my stomach. I'm still surprised that I like the train.

I don't sit down. I prefer tucking myself like a spy in a corner close to any of the exit doors, quietly watching people—mostly entrapped by their phones. Seeing how people miss small opportunities for a friendly chat breaks my heart. They get glued to their devices as if sworn to cancel each other out like noise. Sometime last year, I almost ran over a man fiddling with his phone while strolling across the road!

The only thing I enjoy seeing is that more Black and brown people are on the train than when I came to this country several years ago and felt so out of place, a hare among wolves. There is probably no more multicultural space than on the train. Maybe the public schools. My former neighbour thought it was never good; he griped about keeping cultures pure and whole. I always suspected he meant something else. I never argued with him because he occasionally brought me apples. Once, he gifted me a hefty turkey wrapped in plastic and asked if we ate vultures in Africa.

I smile, remembering him. He died last year.

I keep smiling as I walk by a man older than me.

How's it going? I say, cheerfully, but he looks straight ahead as if I were a speck. Hmm. Maybe things haven't progressed as much as I thought.

A Filipino colleague, whom I haven't seen in the office for some time, once told me how she had overheard her landlady mocking immigrants who swarmed the country like locusts and cooked food that smelled funny.

Maybe this man is related to that landlady.

The Dog

On Floyd Way, I see a nice-looking elderly woman walking her dog. She eyes me as if I were a threat, a bag snatcher. The dog starts snarling as I draw nearer on the sidewalk. For fun, I want to bare my teeth, but I don't because this is the third dog that has behaved aggressively towards me this week.

Hush it, the woman scolds. Hush it, Scout.

The dog bulges his eyes, frothing at the mouth.

The woman looks up. Her eyes flick around.

Hush!

The dog leaps forward, almost dragging the woman sideways—for an instant, I picture her tripping over and banging her head against the curb—but she pulls back the leash. Instead of grunting in pain, the dog growls and claws at the air, and she tightens her grip on the leash, yanking him back from attacking me. Yet the dog keeps leaping back and forth, growling, while she, completely flustered, keeps crying miserably. Stop it, Scout!

I almost dash to the other side of the street. I don't want anyone to feel threatened by me, especially a white woman. To think I am the cause of such agitation. Stepping aside to let them pass, I smile as courteously as I can.

She doesn't smile back, though she goes on hushing Scout.

The dog finally quietens, but he glances back a couple of times, eyeing me coldly, as I continue walking.

I pull my collar tighter and remember a friend who joked about how some white South African farmers had trained their dogs to bark only at Black men. My friend jokes too much. He claims that even animals can be racists.

The Mess

I almost stumble over shoes and boots spilling out of the closet. A jacket is on the floor: my son's. Other jackets perch loosely from the hangers.

I'm home, I say in the doorway.

No one answers.

Then I hear voices in the living room. Wrapped in a blanket on a couch, my wife is watching something on TV. There's a protest in a city, people storming the streets over the killing of another unarmed Black youth.

I lean over, kiss her on the cheek. She doesn't move. She merely grips the remote. Has she been crying?

The kitchen lights are on. Before turning them off, I cringe at the unwashed dishes cluttering the sink. I scratch the back of my neck. My wife is usually fussy about hygiene. What is happening to her these days? She's been sitting in front of the TV most evenings, looking hurt, sad, or distanced.

We argued a few times over her badgering me about things any wife should overlook. She went on about my disarray, as she called it, my dirty boxers stacked in the bedroom closets. I had scolded her for not encouraging our son to go out and make friends; she replied that I didn't know what he must endure as one of only two Black kids in a class of thirty students. If only she ignored certain things.

I sigh and walk upstairs.

I find our son lying in bed. The light is on, as usual.

I have reminded him over a dozen times about saving energy. I showed him our utility bill more than twice. His room is a little dump, pants, shoes, candy wrappers, cookie packets, a half-eaten apple, a crumpled juice box, and toys everywhere. He still needs to learn how to clean up. My wife believes he will grow out of this phase; she likes to remind me that he is only 12.

At 9, I was already ironing my father's clothes. I cooked rice and beans and fried yam, plantain, and fish at that age. Left to my wife, our son would spend the whole day on his desktop, getting more bug-eyed from too much squinting through his thick lens.

I stand there watching him, worried that we are raising him in a way that will break up our marriage eventually—or make him less of a man. I pull the blanket over him, wondering if he still complains to his mother about some classmates wanting to touch his hair.

Running Late

Everyone at the station appears agitated this morning. Except for the ads and news, there are no schedules displayed on the monitors. Times are temporarily unavailable. It stopped snowing last night. A few commuters pack themselves inside the train shelter. Others linger in the station building. Some of us stand behind the yellow line on the platform, waiting.

Above us, a hazy moon. Motley lights spill from the apartment towers across the station. Behind those buildings lies the sprawling Indigenous Peoples Memorial Park, which, occasionally, displays hundreds of empty red dresses on trees. I went there once with my son to remind him of how some fundamentalists had abducted dozens of girls from their schools in Nigeria.

A young girl paces before me, humming. She is wearing

headphones. Her hair is a wild shrub of pink and purple. In a wheelchair, a heavy-set man with a silver beard spilling over his shoulders gazes across at the cars whizzing by. His red baseball cap with an embossed white fox matches his red sweater but not his black joggers and white sneakers. He could pass for Santa Claus. An Arab man is blowing on his cupped hands. Breath clouds flit across his face. He must have lost his gloves.

I don't feel cold, but still, I plunge my hands into my jacket pockets.

Running late again, she says. A woman in her 20s. Is she Korean or Chinese? I can't tell, but she is not Indian.

The train, I mean. It is running late again.

Yeah, I say. Better late than never.

Mm-hmm. She stares at me, winks.

Is she flirting with me?

A train ride is a lifetime. Her voice is almost a whisper, an invitation, like a plate of too-spicy, jerky chicken laid out before me.

I smile with only a light tilt of my lips. We might have something in common. But we both turn as an announcement floats out of an overhead speaker: The next train is arriving now.

Petty Stuff

A semi-trailer truck blares its horn in the distance. In the dimness of our room, I slip quietly into the bed next to my wife. I lie on my left side, press my crotch against her backside, and cup her breast with my right hand. I breathe in her skin and don't smell her perfume. I can't place what she smells like, either.

I move my hand, sliding it down her panties. She doesn't stir. She could be deep asleep. Maybe she is still hurt by our recent fight. What did we even argue about? Petty stuff, I suppose. She will never admit that she always gets emotional over the slightest issue.

She is not getting any apologies from me anytime soon.

I gaze up at the ceiling and wonder if the strange woman at the train station found me attractive.

The Stranger

Snap your fingers. That's how fast you can get friends and followers on social media. And yet, we have grown more disconnected than ever. Which is to say: I don't know where my phone is. I'm glad I can't find it. I used to keep it on my bedside, the first thing I reached for even before I kissed my wife on her brow. I used to wake up at 2 a.m. to check who had retweeted my post or who had liked or commented on my status.

What a relief not to have to check my phone every minute!

The train is bursting with people this evening. Somehow, I can sense an energy like the static you feel in your fingertips when you touch cold metal. Is it coming from the man chomping on a hotdog in the aisle seat, his fingers stained yellow? Usually, my stomach would stir in revolt, I would almost puke, but for some reason, I don't even smell the mustard.

It could be the cold weather. I take a deep breath and wonder what losing one's sense of smell would feel like. I think of my wife's lavender perfume, which always lingered in the air after she had left our apartment. Has she stopped wearing it?

I sense someone staring at me. I turn, and a fat-cheeked baby in a fluffy swaddle blanket, nestled in the crook of his mother's arm, is watching me with eyes the colour of ale. I can't tell exactly if it is a boy or a girl, likely a boy. I smile, thinking his eyes remind me of the craft beer sold at my favourite pub.

The baby's face changes. He is frowning: his forehead pinched tight as if it could read my thoughts. I want to make funny faces, but I stop smiling. The baby begins wriggling in its mother's arm and whimpering as if I have upset it. Humming softly, his mother moves it to her other arm. She rocks her baby gently—perhaps to put it to sleep; still, the baby squirms, squashing his arms against her chest and burrowing its face under the blanket.

I realize that my presence is disturbing the baby. I hope his mother doesn't realize that, too—before she eyeballs me like I am some kind of weirdo—when I hear a stout, furry dog also whimpering at a passenger's feet. The dog ducks her face between her front paws, peering up at me.

Hey. What's the matter, Rico?

The dog continues whimpering.

The owner lowers his hand under the dog's chin, scratching it. Rico, what's that?

I, too, wonder what has gotten into the dog. He looks terrified of something.

It has nothing to do with you, someone says, causing me to flinch.

I see a woman standing next to me. I collect myself immediately. Are you talking to me?

Oh, yeah. You. The newcomer.

Did she recognize me from somewhere? Maybe she wants to bum something off me, but her beige wool coat looks expensive. She seems to be smirking at me. By the way, who is she referring to as the newcomer? I've been living in this country for about a decade.

Do I know you? I try to sound polite because she looks quite familiar. We have met before, haven't we?

Ooh, wow. It feels strange, right? What are the odds of us running into each other again?

What do you mean? I blurt.

She does not seem drunk or stoned. Yet I remember reading in the dailies that several people have been behaving weirdly since the pandemic ended.

Mm, you haven't figured it out yet.

I draw away from her, recognizing her now. The Chinese-looking woman. Could she be interested in me? Did she have a thing for men, dark and well-toned like me?

What are you talking about?

But then she leans forward and picks off lint from my jacket. Her simple, deft gesture embarrasses me. I look around and see that no one has noticed what she just did or is even looking at us. It is as if they couldn't care less about us.

She lifts her head as a voice announces: The next stop is Breonna. Smiling, she says, Like Neo in *The Matrix*, when he sees a black cat walking before him followed by another cat that acts the same way.

You are a strange one, aren't you?

Hey, why are you speaking in a low voice? Look around. Can't you see it yet? No one can hear you. Oh, damn! This is my stop. I don't know how long you're here for, but I hope to see you around. Remember, it has nothing to do with you. It's the vibes. And watch out for the birds! They act freaking scary, too.

The train growls to a halt at Breonna, the upscale neighborhood where I dream of living someday.

Doors normally open on the left.

The strange woman melts into the mass of exiting passengers. As the train glides away towards Regis Trail, I remember the crazy bird I had seen yesterday. Or was it the day before that?

Then the woman winks, without smiling.

Blood/Sirens

Descending the stairs, I realize I last visited the office two or three days ago. Something seems wrong with my memory. It feels as if I need to remember an important detail. Or am I mixing things up? The sounds of shuffling and sharp voices climb the stairs.

I see a tall man roughing up another man, a short fellow in a faded green jacket. At first, I think they are playing games like high school boys, until someone shouts, He's got a knife! I catch a metallic glint and freeze midway. The short man screams; the knife has found his flesh. My legs turn to pillars. The few people waiting for the train disperse like the wind.

The tall man stabs him in the stomach: once, twice, several times, while the short man hugs him clumsily, blocking each thrust with his arms. Each stab wrenches a sharp groan from the short man, who finally flops down, clutching his belly. His assailant flies off into the winter evening. Meanwhile, blood pours out of the writhing body on the floor. I spring down the stairs, careful not to trip headlong, and kneel beside the wounded man.

I regret not having my phone on me.

Help! Somebody help! I scream and scream harder. I want to lay my hands somewhere above his stomach and push like I have seen people do on TV, but I am afraid I might make things worse.

Relief comes over me as I see four or five police officers bursting through the glass doors and racing towards us. They are speaking rapidly to one another while clasping their holsters. The short man is gasping and choking at the same time.

My fingers, sticky with blood, start quivering. The cops will arrest me, thinking I am the assailant—the only Black person close by.

He went that way! I point in the direction the tall man fled. Go after him. He went that way!

Instead, the cops bend over the body, pretending not to hear me. One yaps on his radio, asking if they have dispatched the ambulance. A pair tells a sprinkling of onlookers, who have collected at the entrance and exit doors, to stay back while the fourth cop is telling the bleeding man to hang in there, buddy.

I rise, puzzled that the cops are ignoring me altogether. As if I don't exist. A popular social justice activist once spoke about how Blacks are visible and invisible under the white gaze. Yet, I feel relieved that no one has singled me out.

There is a slight whispering among the onlookers as the cops now stand around the body. They stare at each other, then glance away.

I remain standing there too, horrified because, although I've heard of train station attacks, I have never witnessed one until now. Death is only a minute away, I realize. For some people, less than a minute. I have to get back home at once because I could have been the one stabbed. What am I doing here? I can't remember why I got on the train in the first place. I know there's a popular pub somewhere around this area. Maybe I wanted to sip some beer and have time to think about my family. My wife and son have been ignoring me for the past three or four days. They don't reply when I speak to them. You'd think they've completely lost their hearing. I hope she hasn't turned my son against me.

I make to leave when a paramedical unit arrives at the station. I pause to see whether they can staunch the man's ghastly wounds. One uniformed woman tears something off a pack and puts an oxygen mask on the man's face; another pulls out straps and pads from a portable machine. The man lies on the floor, unmoving—his long toffee hair speckled with his blood. His eyes and lips don't move, either.

Cold air seems to pass through me as though I were a sponge. Everywhere is turning blurry, and I fear I might pass out. Through the blur, I see a freckle-faced young woman peering down into the man's face and taking hold of his wrist.

Someone gasps behind me and asks, What just happened?

I flinch, wondering whether the person has been standing at my back the whole time.

Sorry, Bro. I didn't mean to scare you. What's going on here?

No, you... you... I stutter, dizzy as if I am losing blood.

He flicks his smeared, toffee hair from his cold-bitten face. Are you okay, Bro? he asks, almost snorting.

I glance from his face to the still body the paramedics are lifting off the crimson floor, back at him, and then at the body.

The man jerks around, following my gaze. Ugh, he says, wrinkling his nose. He shivers. What the—Is that—?

A southbound train has just rumbled into view.

—me?

We stare incredulously at each other.

In a flash, I see myself fumbling behind the wheel as a semi-trailer truck veers off the opposite lane, hurtling onto mine—spears of blinding light flood my vision. My car skids off the icy road, banging its rear into concrete, then flipping on its side, and thudding down the craggy ditch. I remember stamping out of our house after fighting over the unflushed toilet with my wife. That was three evenings ago. Across the train station is the pub I was heading to that evening.

Now I stagger back from the man, clutching my chest, as the train chugs away from the same station.

Sirens wail in the distance, strident as glass shattering against metal and rock.

"He went pale,
real pale.
I swear, he looked
like he'd seen
a ghost."

12

TWISTED INTO A SCAPEGOAT

John L. Hill

THEY SAY you never truly understand how quickly life can spiral into hell until it happens to you. For me, it wasn't a single moment but a slow, forsaken descent, like an unseen sickness crawling through your my until one day, it finally knocked me down. My name is Miley Theriault and my life wasn't supposed to end up like this.

Alexander Fletcher. I remember that name well. Too damn well. He acted like royalty in my hometown of Cobourg. It's a quiet little town on the shores of Lake Ontario. Its only problem is that it's hard to find housing. Fletcher was the old man who owned half the town's rental properties, and he was the man they say I killed.

You see, I wasn't always in this cell, surrounded by men who showed the horrors of murder and brutality in their eyes. I wasn't always the guy staring out through iron bars, feeling the crushing weight of a crime I didn't commit pressing down on my chest like a boulder I could never hope to lift. But the story goes back before all that—

I used to have a life. A wife. Two sons. My wife, Coleen, came to this country when she was just a little girl from County Clare in Ireland. Her family had many relatives who had come from Ireland and who had been in the area for more than a hundred years. Coleen's parents, her aunts and uncles and their kids formed an Irish enclave north of town we loved to visit often. I was told that in the 1800s, Irish settlers had emigrated to this part of the world. They had set up a temporary shelter on Cobourg's sandy beach. But the English didn't take kindly to these newcomers, and most of them were driven north of Rice Lake to Peterborough. That's where the in-laws lived.

Both Coleen and I had jobs, and we got along well. We weren't perfect, but we were happy, or at least I thought we were. Then, everything started to unravel when I lost my job at the plant. That's when the drinking began. At first, it was just to numb the disappointment and the guilt of failing my wife and the boys. Then, it was to drown the frustration and shame. But the real disaster? That came later.

Three months behind on rent. Three months of eviction notices piling up like reminders of my failure. The violence happened at home. During an argument, I slapped Coleen. I was out of control. Then the cops took me away. The newspaper reported that Emile Joseph Theriault (criminals always have three names!) had been charged with assault on his wife.

I pleaded guilty, of course. I was saddled with a criminal record. That certainly didn't help my future job prospects. I knew, deep down, I was losing everything.

Coleen left me and took the boys. After the eviction, she and the kids went to live with her mom and dad in Peterborough. That's when I hit rock bottom. I got really drunk.

But none of that would've made me kill a man. Not Alexander Fletcher. Not anybody. And yet, that the old bastard was found dead, stabbed in his office, and somehow, they decided it had to be me. They found me drunk and passed out in a park near where the killing had happened.

Mr. Fletcher did not die instantly. With his last breath, he said, "Tare, E, All." At least, that's what the janitor heard. Sounds a lot like "Theriault," doesn't it? The cops thought so, and that was all they needed.

I wasn't stupid. I knew I'd been set up. But nobody believed me. The jury was fast.

My eviction, my drinking and my admission of a criminal assault on Coleen did not play well with a jury. Four hours to decide my fate. Four hours and my life was gone, sealed behind the bars of Millhaven Penitentiary to begin a life sentence.

The day I met my cellmate, Declan Kelly, I figured him for another tough guy, like most of the inmates here. We didn't talk much at first. It's prison code—don't ask, don't tell. He knew I'd lived in Cobourg but that's about all. But one day, I let it slip. "I'm in for murder," I told him, my voice flat, like it was someone else's story. I didn't expect much of a reaction.

But Declan went pale, real pale. I swear, he looked like he'd seen a ghost. He stared at me for a long second before finally asking, "Was it the old Englishman in Cobourg?" That question stopped me cold. How did he know?

Then he said something that chilled me to my bones. "I know you didn't do it," Declan whispered, his voice barely more than a breath. "Because I know who did."

I felt the blood drain from my face. "How the hell do you know?" My voice was shaky. I didn't trust him—not yet—but I needed to hear what he had to say. Declan leaned in closer. "Because I used to work for them... for the Terry Alt Society."

Now, I don't know what I expected him to say, but that sure as hell wasn't it. He explained it to me—how this secret society went back to the old country, back to Ireland, where they enforced their own twisted form of justice. Landlords, rich men, and anyone they felt wronged the poor, they'd handle it. And when they did, they'd say, "This is for Terry Alt." That's what the killers always said.

It clicked, then. Alexander Fletcher hadn't said my name when he was dying. He wasn't trying to finger me. He was trying to tell the cops who really did it. He was trying to say "Terry Alt."

But they twisted it, twisted me into their scapegoat.

For the first time in years, I had hope. Maybe, just maybe, I could clear my name. Declan told me about a lawyer, Bruce Skinner. Said this guy knew how to work the system, how to fight for the wrongly convicted. I had nothing to lose, so I wrote to Skinner, and to my surprise, he agreed to help. In my phone call with him, I told him how my cellmate used to work for the Terry Alt Society and that he knew who killed Fletcher. I really needed his help. But that's when everything started to go wrong again.

Skinner came to the prison and took my case. He had dug deep into the Terry Alt Society. He told me he had contacted a historical society in Shannon, Ireland, and they had sent him documents about the Terry Alt Society. It had been big in County Clare, especially during the famine. He said it was a secret society formed in Ireland during that time. It died out in that country, and the people he had contacted in Ireland said it didn't exist anymore.

Skinner thought the road was a dead end. Then he did some more digging. He found out there were cold cases in the area. Murders that had gone unsolved. It was like dinosaurs had died out but lived on in an entirely new location. It was possible that the Terry Alt Society continued to carry on here when Irish settlers moved to this country.

He was excited about the findings he made. He thought he had enough ammunition to open up cases the police had given up on. Hell, he thought he might be able to get some international exposure.

But it wasn't all good news. He told me to be very careful. He said he found out about the Terry Alt Society's connections, including how it had infested the prison's social order and how it was not just criminals who manifested its beliefs. Members of this group were now prominent in the area's local government structures, and informants were placed to ensure no word leaked out exposing the society's control methods.

Could the Terry Alt Society be thinking that my cellmate and I were divulging sensitive information crucial to the organization's ongoing existence? Bruce Skinner was sure that prison officials would not know what transpired during the prison visits. Still, he was concerned that I had blurted out too much in my phone call to him. I forgot that those calls are monitored.

If all this information was so dangerous, I asked him how he would go about putting this story together. He didn't give me much of an answer. He mumbled something about trying to appeal my conviction with new evidence and something about bringing a *habeas corpus* application. I didn't question him. I don't really understand a lot of the legal mumbo-jumbo. Bruce Skinner left, saying he would work on a plan to get me freed.

Of course, I told Declan all about what Mr. Skinner had told me. Declan told me that my lawyer was right about keeping everything to myself. It was very dangerous to talk about the Terry Alt Society. He had been a professional hitman before he got caught. He was the only one who had ever been arrested while working for the Terry Alt Society. Even then, he had kept his trap shut about the organization. He told me I should be careful not to repeat anything he or my lawyer had told me. "Loose lips sink ships," he said, and after that conversation, he never opened up to me as he had done before.

But one thing he told me stuck in my brain. My cellmate had stated that when the Terry Alt Society carries out an execution, the killer is required to say out loud that this assassination is being carried out on behalf of Terry Alt.

Getting news is a problem in jail. A newspaper had fallen out of a guard's backpack as he was coming on shift. I picked it up and stuffed it under my shirt. Of course, there was nothing to set off the metal detector as I headed back to my unit. One story in particular caught my attention. The news report read that one night, just a few weeks after I had met with Bruce Skinner, there was a knock at the lawyer's door.

A neighbour had told the local newspaper reporter that he saw a man—big, muscular, someone you wouldn't want to meet in a dark alley—and he heard that man say only one thing before driving a knife into Skinner's chest: "This is for Terry, y'all," or something like that. The speculation was that the killer was probably from the United States. Canadians don't usually say, "Y'all." The paper also said the lawyer's house was ransacked. Police were stymied. Valuables like jewellery and watches were not taken. Police did mention that Skinner's papers, and I assumed everything about my case, were gone. Wiped clean like they never existed.

That was the beginning of the end. The next day, Declan and I were in our cell, talking like we always did. Then, out of nowhere, they came for us. I didn't see their faces, just the flash of steel. They stabbed Declan first. I had never seen a man die before. I watched, and it was like time stood still.

I didn't have time to react before I felt the blade hit my own chest. It was fast. Brutal. Then I heard the words: "For Terry Alt." They shoved the blade even deeper. But it wasn't the pain that scared me most. It was the silence that followed. They cut out our tongues. They didn't want us to talk. Ever.

The local paper ran the story. Said two inmates were found dead, stabbed in their cells. No big deal. Prison life. But they didn't know the truth. They didn't know what we'd uncovered, or how deep this thing really went.

As I lay there, bleeding out on that cold cell floor, I thought about my wife, Coleen. About my boys. I'd never see them again. Never tell them the truth. But worse than that... worse than death itself... was knowing that the Terry Alt Society was still out there. Still in control. And no one would ever know the real story.

Because the dead don't talk.

"There was less blood and more noise than he had expected."

13

MARTYR'S RECKONING

James R. Parker

RICHARD stood amidst the acrid smells of sweat, gasoline, and the lingering coppery odour of blood. He could hear their prayers and curses, he could hear the clang of his hammer on the nail as he drove it into the hard wood. And he could hear the screaming of his victim.

He was finished. The nail was a few inches deep into the timber and still extended an inch above the wrist of the unfortunate man tied to it. He stood and stepped back. The others were finished too. Two crosses were raised by ropes to be upright. The men screamed again as the crosses thumped into the holes that had been dug at their base. It was Richard's first crucifixion, and there was less blood and more noise than he had expected.

He stepped back farther and examined his work. The men on the crosses were not screaming now but gasping and moaning. The only words he could understand were pleas to be let down, begging for it to end. The rest was unintelligible.

"Your first one?" a voice behind him asked. He turned and saw Noah, his unit commander, looking at him, appraising him as always.

"Yes," he replied. Then: "How long does it—ah—take, usually?"

Noah shrugged, lighting a cigarette. "It varies," he said, waving his hand. "It depends on what kind of shape they're in. These are soldiers. It could be some hours.

"Not as much blood as I thought," Richard murmured.

"They don't bleed to death," Noah replied, exhaling smoke. "They suffocate, or their hearts give out. It's not about blood—it's about the message. Watch, and you'll understand."

One of the soldiers lifted himself on his arms, screeched, and fell back. The crowd cheered and hissed. Richard was mentally divided on this event. Yes, the prisoner deserved death for his actions. But, on the other hand, would he put an animal through this? Would he torture a dog? There were rules on how to butcher animals for meat; surely there must be rules on how prisoners should be executed. It was beyond him, though. He turned away from the gruesome scene just before another cheer rose from the crowd.

He turned from the spectacle and pushed his way through the crowd, seeking the relative silence of his quarters.

The cot creaked beneath Richard as he lay back, staring at the low ceiling. The shouts and cheers outside felt distant now, though the screams still echoed in his ears.

He did not think he was a very smart man, and generally left profound thoughts to those better equipped. Still, was it wrong to question one's role? Perhaps he should ask. He was thinking about this when he passed into a disturbed sleep, fractured by uneasy dreams of crosses and blood.

The air was cooler when Richard awoke, though the brightness of the day quickly burned away that reprieve. He sat up and yawned, his concerns of earlier forgotten. Outside the tent, the day was bright and still hot. He made his way to the area where he knew coffee could be found.

On his way out he saw Noah, who gripped Richard's arm with a firm but friendly hand.

"You did well yesterday," Noah began. "But I saw your face. You felt sorry for that guy, didn't you?"

Richard hesitated. "I don't think it was pity," he said carefully. "It's just… the screaming, the blood. I'm not sure I'm cut out for this kind of thing."

Noah frowned. "Perhaps some time in combat. See what these mercenaries do to your friends and family. You will return a different man. Would you like that? There is a push on some villages nearby; I could arrange to get you there."

"I'm not much of a fighter," Richard replied, looking at the ground. "I'm not sure I'm any good at this."

"That's for me to decide," Noah said with a faint smirk. "Come to my tent after dinner. We'll talk about your next steps."

Richard had more to say, but turned away and decided to go to his work space and perhaps get a few things done. He worked in one of the few buildings with real walls, concrete ones, and the space had a degree of air conditioning. That wasn't for him, though; it was for the computers. He did accounting work, keeping track of resources needed at the various combat zones and helping keep this headquarters fed.

He sat at a battered desk, his hands resting on an old typewriter. The rhythmic clatter of the keys as he tallied supplies—flour, ammunition, fuel—was a strange comfort. It was a task he could complete without thinking, one that allowed his mind to drift.

He stared at the rows of numbers, the stark simplicity of the ledger contrasting with the chaos outside. He couldn't shake the image of the crosses, the screams. Was this really the justice he'd fought for? Or was it something else entirely?

Row after row of numbers, representing ammunition, flour, gasoline, cash accounts and a host of other important items flowed through his keyboard and, when he saved them, out to their remote storage sites. His friend James came by and sat at his own cubicle but said nothing. That suited Richard, he wanted to be alone. More typing, more data. An hour went by without notice. Then another. He was working as if in a trance, not really seeing what he was doing, moving on instinct. Click, click, enter.

"Just get through today," he muttered to himself, typing the next row.

Time slipped by in a haze of numbers and monotony. Then, "Wham"— a deafening roar shattered the stillness. The noise and compression blast hit him at the same time and knocked him to the floor. He shook his head and sat up, confused. James was running for the door. He should too, he thought. He staggered to his feet and moved unsteadily in the same direction that he recalled James had been running. As he approached the brightly lit doorway he could see James racing toward the concealed door to the shelter across the compound. Richard saw the bright glare of the blast, felt the heat, and was again knocked to the ground. But he also saw James sliced to pieces and set afire by that government bomb. Something smacked him hard on the forehead before everything got dark.

Richard returned slowly to the world, hearing vague sounds and then voices. His eyelids fluttered and then opened, but he was unable to move otherwise. It was still light, and he seemed to be in his tent, in his own cot. He tried to sit up and groaned, then fell back. His head hurt. Someone touched his arm.

"Richard, can you hear me?" a voice asked gently.

"Yes," he mumbled. "I can hear."

"What is your name?"

"Richard. What happened? Where is James?" Everything seemed to be moving too slowly.

"Do you know where you are?"

"Camp B-12," Richard replied. "James. I saw—"

The voice hesitated. "I'm sorry. James didn't make it."

Richard's chest tightened, but he said nothing.

"You've got a concussion," the voice continued. "You'll recover, but you need to rest. Try to rest but not sleep, if that's possible."

Footsteps retreated, leaving Richard alone with the muffled sounds of the camp. Outside, men shouted instructions as they sifted through the wreckage, the air thick with smoke and grief. Richard closed his eyes, but the image of James lingered—his colleague reduced to fragments in an instant.

James had been sharp, calm under pressure, the one everyone relied on to untangle problems no one else could solve. Now, he was gone, just another casualty of the fight.

Hours passed in a blur of pain and restless thoughts. The tent darkened with the setting sun, and the noise outside began to fade. A figure entered, and Richard turned his head to see Noah sitting beside him.

"Richard," Noah said quietly. "You awake?"

"I'm alive," Richard muttered. "How's the camp?"

"It's a mess, but we'll manage. They were after our munitions, and they got most of them. Not all." Noah's gaze darkened. "We lost ten men today, including James."

Richard nodded stiffly. "He was a good man. One of the best."

"Hard worker, too," Noah said. "A real loss." He paused, lighting a cigarette. "Richard, I was going to talk to you tonight about joining a combat unit, but I've got something else in mind now."

Richard frowned. "What is it?"

"You don't have much family left, do you? Just your sister, Julia?"

"That's right."

"How do you feel about the people who did this?" Noah asked, his voice low and even.

Richard's jaw tightened. "I would harm them. Kill them. But what can I do, I'm only one man and a poor soldier. What can I do?"

Noah smiled faintly. "I'm sending a team into the city to teach them a lesson. Explosives. You'd be helping strike back at the ones who did this."

Richard hesitated, the weight of the offer pressing down on him. A mission like that meant no return. He knew it, and so did Noah. Still, what did he have left to give but his life? Hadn't he already offered it, by being here?

"I'll do it," he said finally.

Noah nodded. "Good. Rest for now. We'll talk details when you're feeling better."

As Noah left, Richard stared at the darkened ceiling. His mind buzzed with thoughts of James, of the men they'd lost, and of the future he couldn't quite picture.

The next few days passed in a haze of sleep, cold compresses, and medication. The doctor visited frequently, ensuring Richard's concussion was improving. By the end of the week, he was walking again, eating regular meals, and regaining his strength. He thought often of Noah's offer. The fear of dying lingered, but it seemed a simpler, cleaner end than the bloody tasks he had witnessed.

One morning, Richard received a note from Noah, summoning him to breakfast. When Richard arrived, Noah was seated with four others. He waved Richard over.

"Good. You're here," Noah said as Richard sat. "These are your teammates. You don't need to know each other—talk later if you want. For now, listen."

Noah tore a piece of bread and began to speak, his tone casual but firm. "The ones responsible for last week's attack live in the city. They weren't the ones who carried it out, but without them, James and the others would still be alive. You'll drive into the city and park at designated spots. The cars will be loaded with explosives and shrapnel—standard setup. You'll each receive a target location and a time. When the moment comes, you detonate. If anything disrupts the plan, you'll get a call with new instructions."

One of the others spoke, his voice shaky, "How can you be sure they'll be there?"

"The intel is solid," Noah replied. "You'll have phones and backup plans. Just stick to the timing."

There were no further questions. Noah stood, brushing crumbs off his lap. "We meet here tomorrow at noon. Be ready. And remember, this isn't just about revenge. It's about sending a message."

Noon came faster than Richard expected. He arrived early but had no appetite. The others were already there, sitting in uneasy silence. One man, short and wiry, devoured a plate of food with mechanical efficiency.

Richard poured himself coffee and sat down. "Hi," he ventured. "I'm Richard."

The man barely glanced at him. "I know. Let's keep this professional, yeah?" He stood, carrying his plate to fetch more food.

Noah entered with the others, breaking the tense silence. "Richard!" he called. "Not eating? Or done already?"

"I'm fine," Richard said, holding up his cup.

"Good. You'll have time for dinner in town before the mission," Noah replied with a grin. "Make the most of every chance, don't you think?"

The group gathered around the table as Noah unrolled maps and schedules. "Two of you will target the theatre.

Two will be in cars. The targets will be at the theatre for a screening. If all goes well, it'll be over quickly."

The briefing was brisk. Maps, routes, and timing were clear, leaving no room for error. Afterwards, Richard was handed the keys to an old Ford. It was a sturdy car, though its interior was crudely altered to house 400 kilograms of explosives mixed with nails and scrap metal.

As Richard started the engine, Noah leaned in through the window. "Safe journey, my friend. I'll be joining you soon enough." He clapped Richard on the shoulder and stepped back.

The pre-programmed GPS guided Richard through the countryside. The other car turned off early, leaving him alone. The outskirts loomed ahead, a city scarred by years of conflict; the streets were barely recognizable—craters, rubble, and barricades replaced landmarks he once knew.

He parked near a café that had survived the worst of the destruction. Despite his lack of hunger, he ordered a meal—a plate of stew and bread, along with a pudding. The food reminded him of his mother, of simpler times before the war consumed his life. He barely touched the food but left a generous tip, everything he had left.

As he stepped back into the car, the weight of what lay ahead settled fully onto his shoulders.

The GPS guided Richard to the hotel. Without it, he might have been lost in the maze of the bomb-scarred streets. The Ford's clock read 6:21 p.m.—the time set for detonation. He couldn't park too early, so he drove aimlessly, circling the target area to avoid suspicion.

At 6:45, he pulled up near the entrance and cut the engine. The scene was deceptively ordinary. A young man played guitar by the museum steps across the street. A bus unloaded children nearby; two men sat on the grass, a chessboard between them.

His hand hovered over the detonator on the passenger seat. He sighed and grasped it firmly, squeezing before doubt could take hold.

What came next was not what Richard expected. He expected a loud noise, a bright light, heat, a moment of pain before... well, before whatever would happen next. He did get the bright light, and a moment of noise, but nothing else. It was as if the world were very calm, silent. He tried to move his head to see the street but found that he could not. He could not move at all.

No blinding flash, no roar, no searing heat. Instead, everything froze. The world around him was eerily still, as if turned to stone.

He strained to move, but his body refused to obey. His eyes could shift slightly, giving him glimpses of the frozen world: the guitarist, paused mid-strum; the chess players, staring intently at their pieces; the children, laughing and frozen in motion as they stepped off the bus. Even a scrap of paper hung suspended in mid-air.

He wanted to shout, to scream, but he could make no sound. This frightened him more than anything else. How could he ask for help? And who could help him? The statues around his car? What sort of weapon had they given him? The panic welled up and he again tried to scream "What is happening?" He looked around again for any motion, strained for any sound. "Oh God," he cried in his mind, "Help me."

"A very appropriate sentiment", responded a voice. It was a man's voice, a very clear, unaccented baritone.

"Thank God!" Richard tried to shout. "Can you help me? Where are you?"

"I am near," the voice said. "But there is a limit to what I can do to help you. Or to what I'd want to do, actually. You have been a bad man, haven't you?"

"No!" Richard thought back fiercely. "I'm a soldier! I fight for my people. I've given everything for the cause, and now my life!"

The scene shifted abruptly, and Richard was back at the warehouse, hammering a nail into a plank during last week's crucifixion. He could again hear the clang of his hammer on the nail as he drove it into the hard wood. He could hear the hammering of the others, smell the blood, see and feel the heat.

"Is this your war?" the voice asked as the scene faded. "Is this the action of a warrior? To me, it would seem not, but I am not your judge."

Richard was back in the car, immobilized. "This doesn't look like courage to me."

"I just follow orders," Richard stammered. "I am of low rank. I'm not smart or educated. I did what I was told, like any soldier."

"Here is something to consider," said the voice, still calm. "Who is this Noah person to tell you what to do? Have you not been given free will? Have you no understanding of what is right for a man to do, and what is not?"

"My commander—Noah—he said it was necessary. That it was for the greater good."

"And yet here you are, a martyr," the voice said coldly. "Dead because of those orders. Whether by betrayal or blind obedience, you've met the same end."

Richard was confused but still had the words and convictions he had been taught. "But I die for a purpose, in battle against the oppressors and those who would harm my people."

The voice softened. "Look around. Do you see soldiers?"

Richard's gaze shifted to the street. The guitarist, the laughing children, the elderly couple holding hands on a bench—none of them fit the image of an enemy.

"They're all enemies of my people," Richard said weakly.

"Fool!" the voice boomed. "What do you know of their lives? Did they raise arms against you? Or were they just living their lives as you once lived yours? Who are you to judge who should live and who should die?"

The voice paused, letting the weight of its words settle. "You chose this path. Perhaps you were misled, but deep down, you knew. You questioned. You hesitated. And yet you continued."

Richard thought for a while. Surrender seemed a good choice. "There are no soldiers," he said. "But I was told—"

"You chose to do the things you did. Perhaps you were misled about some things, but you knew that there was something wrong. You knew that your treatment of the captured soldiers and the refugee women and the innocent civilians in the schools and hospitals you bombed were not soldiers, and you wondered about the morality of killing them. You asked yourself whether it was right to do those things. And so you are here, and your answer must have been that it was right. What do you say?"

Richard's anger flared. "Where is this place? Who are you? Are you judging me? Only God can do that—and only after I die!"

"Good questions, but I will answer them in an order that I will choose. First, you are dead. You died when you pressed the button that set off the bomb in your car. Here is more interesting: We have created an entire Universe for you. A tiny one, certainly; you can see most of it. It is a representation of the place where your bomb exploded. Very accurate, is it not?"

"Dead?" Richard's thoughts spiralled. "I'm dead?"

"Of course. Was that not the point? This was your choice, your plan. You sought martyrdom. Why does this surprise you?"

"Because I was promised fair judgement. Or oblivion, at least." Richard's panic deepened. "Is this still my home?"

"Yes and no. It's the street you died on, frozen in time. And judgement? It has already happened."

"Then why am I here? What was this judgement?"

"You've been judged for every action, every thought, every excuse—it's all known. Forgiveness requires repentance while alive. You never sought it. Now, let me ask you something: have you thought of the soldiers you have killed since you died?"

Richard hesitated. "What do they matter? They were the oppressors."

"Were they?" the voice pressed. "Look at them again."

Richard's neck and arm began to tingle, as though waking from numbness. "Who are you?" he demanded. "The Satan?"

The voice chuckled. "Everyone wants to meet the Satan. No, I'm not him. I am Olivier, a guide for those judged for their sins. My role is to help you understand your situation. I've done this for two thousand years, but my time on Earth is ending."

"So, you're here to take me to Heaven?" Richard asked, though he already knew the answer.

"You still don't understand. You will not enter Heaven. Your life has been weighed, and you've been found wanting. You murdered innocents and took your own life. Heaven is not your destination. This"—the voice paused—"this is your eternity."

The tingling in Richard's neck grew sharper, turning into heat. His ear burned. "I didn't commit suicide," he insisted. "I fought for my people!"

"You pressed the detonator knowing you would die. That is suicide. Worse, the lives you took were not soldiers. The elderly couple by your car, the children on the bus—none of them had harmed you or your cause. They were innocent. And you knew this."

The scene shifted again. Richard stood at the site of the crucifixion, hammering nails into a young soldier's hands. He saw the man's terror, his tears, the way he begged not for himself but for his family. For the first time, Richard noticed the soldier's youth—barely more than a boy.

The voice interrupted his thoughts. "This man was 19 years old. His name was Sean. He was drafted into the army, sent far from his home. He didn't choose this war, Richard, just as you didn't choose to be born into yours. He wrote a letter to his mother the night before you crucified him. He told her he wanted to come home and study medicine. That's the life you took."

The scene faded, replaced by the street of the explosion. Frozen in time, Richard saw an enemy soldier across the street, reaching out to shield a child from the blast. The soldier's expression was one of pure instinct, a reflex to protect rather than harm.

"They both survived the blast. The child is fine, but the soldier lost both legs. He will never walk again, yet he forgives you. He told reporters, 'We all make mistakes in war. I hope, one day, whoever planted that bomb finds peace.'"

Richard's throat tightened. "He forgives me? After what I did?"

"Yes," the voice said simply. "Now, can you forgive them?"

"I don't know," Richard admitted. "I've hated those enemies my whole life. They killed my father, my friends—"

"And how many fathers, sons, and friends have you killed?" the voice interrupted sharply. "The soldiers you hate were told the same lies you were. That they fought for justice. That they were defending their people. Does that sound familiar?"

The tingling in Richard's neck returned, stronger now, but his focus stayed on the frozen scene around him. He saw the humanity in the faces of the soldiers, the fear and exhaustion that mirrored his own.

"I didn't know," he whispered.

"You didn't want to know," the voice replied, its tone softer now. "Hatred blinds, and a part of my job was to blind you. Hate and fear make monsters out of men, stripping them of their humanity in your eyes. Yet here they are: human, as you are. Will you choose to see them, now?"

"I... I do," Richard said, his voice breaking. "I see them."

The voice paused, as though considering. "It changes nothing about your fate, Richard. But perhaps it will change something about you."

Richard's fate remained grim: to live out the final seconds of his life endlessly, each day a repeat of the same moment of destruction. Yet the voice left him with the gift of memory—fragments of these reflections that resurfaced each day. As Richard's eternity stretched on, he found himself returning to those faces: the young soldier begging for mercy, the protector shielding the child, the humanity in those he once saw as enemies.

The voice returned to its steady, calm tone. "You understand now, don't you? Hatred—yours, theirs, anyone's—is a cycle. It destroys lives on all sides. But you chose to perpetuate it. You ignored the humanity of those you harmed."

"I see them now," Richard whispered, the weight of realization crushing him. "The soldiers, the children... I see them. I was wrong."

The voice paused, its tone softening. "It is good that you see this. But understanding must come in life to change your course. You chose this path, and your fate is sealed. Eternity does not forgive, Richard. For all gods, taking your own life is wrong—it was a gift, and you rejected it. The punishment for you is to relive that moment forever."

Richard's throat tightened as the tingling in his neck turned to searing heat. "But if I see now, doesn't that matter? Can't it count for something? I have been evil, I know that now. I repent. What will it serve to punish me like this? I can't use anything I learn; I am dead. Please, in God's name."

"You know why. But, unlike me, you are eternal. That was your gift, but also it can be a punishment. All humans live forever, or so it will appear to them. You will live only one day, the same day, forever. You will, however, not remember all of the days, only the one you are living in. For you it's the only day there is. You will begin each day wondering where you are, we will have this discussion, and you will end the day in small bloody pieces all over the square."

"Yet, it is possible that the universe is not done with you. Perhaps the echoes of your understanding will ripple beyond this loop. But that is not for me to know."

"And now," the voice said, calm again, "I must go. Your device exploded microseconds ago. The sensations you are feeling in your neck and ear are small pieces of hot metal from that device." The voice was getting fainter. "Well, I have another Universe to create. I would say 'farewell,' but 'goodbye' is more appropriate."

"Wait," Richard screamed in his mind, "If I won't remember any other day, then has this happened before? Is this the… how many times?"

"Interesting question," said the voice. Then, the voice was gone.

PART TWO

SIGNALS FROM THE DEPARTED

Timeless Tales

~ 14 ~

PARANORMAL ENCOUNTERS

Samuel de Champlain et al

THESE STORIES take you deep into the uncharted wilderness of the North, where early explorers ventured into lands steeped in the medicine and magic of the Indigenous Peoples. Drawn from authentic journal entries, they reveal moments of awe and wonder—but also encounters with the unknown. In these accounts, the ice holds secrets, sounds carry warnings, and the line between the natural and the supernatural blurs. These are tales of bravery, conflict, and the chilling consequences of the paranormal in a world few dared to enter.

Samuel de Champlain

Champlain's Journal Entry, 1609: *"Traveling through the forests near the Great Lakes, one could not help but feel the immense solitude. The trees, ancient and towering, seemed to whisper secrets to one another as we passed. There was a strange sound that followed us—a crackling or rustling—that the men said was only the wind. Yet, I felt as though unseen eyes were watching from the forest, a sensation I could not shake even as I lay by the fire that night."*

Known as the "Father of New France," Samuel de Champlain not only forged alliances with Indigenous Nations but also documented moments of mystery during his travels.

Journal Entry, 1613: *"In the village of the Algonquin people, I observed with great curiosity their ceremonies of appeasement to the spirits of the land and water. They sang songs in a tongue unfamiliar to me, their voices rising and falling in haunting cadence. The chief explained to me through my interpreter that these were offerings to the guardian of the river, a spirit that, if angered, could overturn canoes and drown men in its fury. I smiled at the idea, but that night, as the wind howled through the pines and the river's surface churned in the moonlight, I wondered if their tales held more truth than my reason could allow."*

These accounts reveal how Champlain, a man of reason and exploration, confronted the mystical and unexplained forces of the New World, blurring the line between belief and skepticism.

Henry Hudson

Henry Hudson, the intrepid English navigator, is renowned for his explorations of the Arctic in the early 1600s. Accounts from Hudson and his crew touch upon the supernatural and mysterious.

Hudson's Journal Entry, 1608: *"This morning, one of our company, looking overboard, saw a mermaid; and calling up some of the company to see her, one more came up, and by that time she had come close to the ship's side, looking earnestly on the men: a little after, a sea came and overturned her. From the navel upward, her back and breasts were like a woman's... her body as big as one of us; her skin very white; and long hair hanging down behind, of colour black."*

Crew member Abacuck Prickett's Journal Entry, 1611: *"The ice was so thick that we could not get through, and the cold so extreme that our men could scarcely endure it. Yet, by the will of God, we made our way; but at length, our victuals failing, and our men being sore pinched with hunger, we lost our courage."*

The journals of Henry Hudson and his crew provide a window into the challenges and mysteries of early Arctic and subarctic exploration, touching upon experiences that evoke the supernatural, reflecting awe and trepidation.

David Thompson

Journal Entry, 1811: *"I saw the track of a large Animal—has 4 large Toes about 3 or 4 Inches long & a small nail at the end of each. The Ball of his foot sank about 3 Inches deeper than his Toes—the hinder part of his foot did not mark well. The whole is about 14 Inches long by 8 Inches wide & very much resembles a large Bear's Track. It was in the Rivulet in about 6 Inches snow."*

Explorer David Thompson documented his journeys meticulously as he explored the land that is now Canada.

The journal entry was documented on January 7, 1811, while he and his party were attempting to cross the Rocky Mountains near present-day Jasper, Alberta. They had come across strange tracks in the snow.

Forty years later, around 1850, Thompson revisited this encounter with added reflection:

"Continuing our journey in the afternoon, we came on the track of a large animal, the snow about six inches deep on the ice; I measured it; four large toes each of four inches in length, to each a short claw; the ball of the foot sunk three inches lower than the toes.

"The hinder part of the foot did not mark well, the length fourteen inches, by eight inches in breadth, walking from north to south, and having passed about six hours. We were in no humour to follow him; the Men and Indians would have it to be a young mammoth, and I held it to be the track of a large old grizzly bear; yet the shortness of the nails, the ball of the foot, and its great size was not that of a Bear, otherwise that of a very large old Bear, his claws worn away, the Indians would not allow."

Oral history from Thompson's First Nations guides records evidence that they knew about these huge creatures and respected their ways. On this matter, he wrote:

"Reports from old times had made the head branches of this River, and the Mountains in the vicinity, the abode of one, or more, very large animals, to which I never appeared to give credence; for these reports appeared to arise from that fondness for the marvellous so common to mankind: but the sight of the track of that large a beast staggered me, and I often thought of it, yet never could

bring myself to believe such an animal existed. I thought it might be the track of some Monster Bear."

In addition to the "monster bear" occurrences, David Thompson wrote in his journal about the guides' deep connection to their land and their reverence for natural sites, which they believed were inhabited by powerful spirits. He told of their beliefs that mountains and rivers were the abodes of guardian spirits, and engaging with these sites required adherence to traditional rituals to ensure harmony and balance.

Lewis and Clark

At about the same time in history, in the early 1800s, Meriwether Lewis and William Clark were traversing similar terrain in what is now Montana and Idaho. On their journey, they camped in remote wilderness locations and documented hearing unexplained noises during the night. On September 17, 1804, Clark noted:

Clark's Journal Entry, 1804: *"Last night we were all alarmed by a large rustling noise among the bushes, proceeded by a loud noise, like a growl, and some whistles, and a noise like a dog, we could not see what it was owing to the dark night, but all prepared themselves for action, and remained quiet for some time, nothing more was heard of it."*

Lewis and Clark were also familiar with their guides' spiritual practices. On April 22, 1805, Lewis reflected on his sense of wonder and reverence for the natural world:

Lewis's Journal Entry, 1805:"*This evening we witnessed a most beautiful sunset, the clouds which had passed during the day had dispersed, and the horizon was clear, except a few light clouds which appeared to have been purified by the genius of tranquility."*

Drawing inspiration from these journal entries, one might imagine a narrative where the unexplained nocturnal noises are attributed to mythical creatures of Indigenous folklore, or where the explorers' encounters with Indigenous spiritual beliefs lead to mysterious or unexplainable events.

Sir John Franklin

Many explorers, including those featured in this story, have inspired films and television series. While many of these depictions draw from authentic journal entries, they are often creatively reinterpreted for various reasons.

For example, the case of Sir John Franklin has sparked fascination through the dramatized productions of the television series *The Terror,* which told of his Arctic expeditions—with a supernatural twist. In reality, Franklin's journals from his expeditions focus mostly on practical observations and survival rather than explicit descriptions of supernatural or eerie events.

Franklin's Journal Entries, real and imagined:

Here are a few of his journal entries from 1821 to 1845 followed by creative interpretations as though Franklin himself were documenting his eerie experiences.

Journal Entry, 1821: *"The luminous appearances in the heavens cast an extraordinary light over the snow-clad landscape, unlike any we had encountered before."*

Creative Interpretation: *"The aurora borealis tonight defies all earthly description. Great curtains of light unfurl across the heavens, their eerie green hues dancing like spectres on a celestial stage. I hear whispers—though the men insist it is the wind—and my skin prickles with a sense of foreboding. One of the crew, a man of staunch courage, claimed he saw figures moving within the lights, pale shapes that beckoned silently. I laughed it off to steady the others, but I feel it in my marrow: the Arctic holds secrets not meant for men."*

Journal Entry, approx. 1845: *"The desolation stretches beyond the eye's reach, a reminder of nature's unyielding dominion over man."**

Creative Interpretation: *The ice has locked us in its unrelenting grip. A sailor fell ill last night, raving about shadows moving on the ice, their shapes human yet twisted, stretching unnaturally against the moonlight. I visited him at dawn, and his face was as pale as the snow outside. He spoke of a voice that whispered his name, drawing him toward the vast, frozen void. We chalk it up to the sickness, but I feel the air grow heavier with each passing hour.*

At midnight, I ventured out alone, seeking solace from the oppressive confines of the ship. The cold was biting, but it was not the chill that gripped my heart—it was the sound.

A faint, melodic hum rose from the distance, like a lament sung by unseen mourners. I could not pinpoint its source, but it seemed to seep from the very ice beneath my boots. I returned to the ship, and the hum ceased, though I felt it resonating within me long after.

History implies that during the searches for Franklin's lost expedition, Inuit witnesses told of seeing disoriented white men in the Arctic and spoke of malevolent spirits (known as *Torngarsuk*) in the region. This account was not recorded by Franklin himself but by search parties.

Creative Interpretation: *"An Inuit man brought news today, though I am unsure whether to call it a warning. He described white men moving across the tundra, their eyes hollow and their steps unsteady. "Their souls are not with them," he said, gesturing toward the sky. "They walk, but they are not alive." I cannot fathom what he means, but the crew is unnerved. I have seen their glances, the way they linger on the shadows stretching too long in the dim Arctic light.*

"Today, we encountered an Inuit family near the frozen strait. They spoke of a spirit called Torngarsuk that guards these lands, unseen but ever-present. When I pressed for more, the elder's gaze turned distant, his voice low as he described a creature neither man nor beast. "Respect the ice," he said, "or it will claim you." His words lingered, heavy as the frost, and I find myself looking over my shoulder more often than I care to admit."

Final Entry, Imagined: *"The silence here is alive. It presses against us, heavy and unyielding. Last night, I dreamed of a figure cloaked in frost, standing at the edge of the camp. It watched me with eyes that glimmered like stars caught in ice. When I awoke, the dream felt more real than the waking world. I wonder now if the Arctic itself watches us, not as a passive observer, but as something ancient and sentient. If I do not write again, let this serve as my warning to those who follow: this land is not ours. We trespass upon a realm we cannot understand."*

These reimagined journal entries frame Franklin's experiences as encounters with the supernatural, drawing on historical accounts and Inuit lore to add depth.

Alexander Mackenzie

Scottish explorer Alexander Mackenzie played a major role in settler exploration of the North. His expeditions, including along the Dehcho (Mackenzie) River in 1789, were driven by his belief that it might lead to such a passage or a western route to the Pacific Ocean.

However brilliant his navigation skills were, his Dene guides did not hold a good opinion of Mackenzie. They called him "Long Neck" for reasons unknown. In Dene culture, people worked together, including canoeing on the Dehcho, so they were contemptuous of Mackenzie. They observed him to be simply "sitting in the boat being paddled around like a King." According to Dene oral recollections, it was "unusual for them to run into that kind of personality."

MacKenzie's Journal Entries, Real and Imagined

Journal Entry, 1793: *"The natives... assembled about us in great numbers, and were in a state of extreme agitation and alarm. They immediately began to rub us with their hands, and to blow upon us, as a ceremony necessary to secure us from any danger or mischief."*

Creative Interpretation: *"The natives gathered around us in great numbers, their agitation unmistakable. Their movements were deliberate, hands reaching out to touch us, their breaths warm as they blew gently upon us. It was not aggression but a ritual, a protective ceremony born of deep belief. I stood still, uncertain, as they worked with an intensity that suggested forces beyond my understanding. Their eyes held both fear and purpose, as though they sought to shield us from dangers I could neither see nor comprehend. When they finished, the air was heavy with silence, and I felt the weight of their unspoken warnings."*

Journal Entry, 1793: *"About twelve, we came to the foot of a mountain... from which a subterraneous noise proceeded that resembled the distant firing of cannon."*

Creative Interpretation: *"As we approached the mountain at midday, an unnatural stillness settled over the landscape. Then came the sound—a deep, rumbling noise that seemed to rise from the very heart of the earth. It rolled out in intervals, distant yet thunderous, like the muffled firing of great cannons.*

"The men paused, their eyes scanning the rock face as though seeking a source for the unearthly echo. But there was nothing—no visible movement, no wind, only the sound reverberating through the wilderness. I could feel its weight in my chest, an unspoken warning from the mountain itself, guarding secrets we dared not disturb."

The explorers in this story—Samuel de Champlain, David Thompson, Lewis and Clark, Henry Hudson, John Franklin, and Alexander Mackenzie—made incredible journeys through unknown lands. They showed bravery and determination as they mapped new routes and expanded European knowledge of these regions. But their expeditions also brought them face-to-face with the unexplainable.

In the frozen wilderness, far from familiar civilization, the paranormal lurked—strange lights in the sky, unnatural sounds in the night, and a palpable sense of being watched by forces they could not comprehend. These lands, deeply connected to the medicine and magic of the Indigenous Peoples, were not merely uncharted—they were fiercely protected, imbued with power and mystery. For the explorers, the wilderness held not only the threat of the cold and the unknown but also the unnerving sense that they had entered a realm where they did not belong.

15

THE HORROR *of* FRANKENSTEIN

Mary Shelley

It was on a dreary night of November that I beheld the accomplishment of my toils. With an anxiety that almost amounted to agony, I collected the instruments of life around me, that I might infuse a spark of being into the lifeless thing that lay at my feet. It was already one in the morning; the rain pattered dismally against the panes, and my candle was nearly burnt out, when, by the glimmer of the half-extinguished light, I saw the dull yellow eye of the creature open; it breathed hard, and a convulsive motion agitated its limbs.

How can I describe my emotions at this catastrophe, or how delineate the wretch whom, with such infinite pains and care, I had endeavoured to form? His limbs were in proportion, and I had selected his features as beautiful. Beautiful!—Great God! His yellow skin scarcely covered the work of muscles and arteries beneath; his hair was of a lustrous black, and flowing; his teeth of a pearly whiteness; but these luxuriances only formed a more horrid contrast with his watery eyes, that seemed almost of the same colour as the dun white sockets in which they were set, his shrivelled complexion, and straight black lips.

The different accidents of life are not so changeable as the feelings of human nature. I had worked hard for nearly two years, for the sole purpose of infusing life into an inanimate body. For this I had deprived myself of rest and health. I had desired it with an ardour that far exceeded moderation; but now that I had finished, the beauty of the dream vanished, and breathless horror and disgust filled my heart. Unable to endure the aspect of the being I had created, I rushed out of the room, and continued a long time traversing my bedchamber, unable to compose my mind to sleep.

The very thought of the room where the creature stirred filled me with dread. I paced feverishly, replaying the scene in my mind. The flicker of the candlelight, the rise and fall of the wretch's chest, the grotesque twitch of his limbs—these images imprinted themselves on my mind as vividly as if I still stood before him.

Aside, Reflection

Before this night, my mind had been consumed by my work—an all-encompassing obsession that had alienated me from the world. Now, as I paced the room, my thoughts drifted back to the years I had spent in relentless pursuit of this creation.

From the moment I first conceived the idea of bestowing animation upon lifeless matter, my thoughts had been deeply engaged in one pursuit. I pursued my undertaking with unrelaxed and breathless eagerness. My mind was filled with one thought, one conception, one purpose. So deeply was I engrossed in it that I often neglected my studies, my family, and my friends. I seemed to have lost all soul or sensation but for this one pursuit.

And the results of this obsessive labour were not limited to the psychological. I grew pale with study and emaciated by confinement. Often, I had worked through the night, ignoring the call of hunger or exhaustion. By the dim light of my lamp, I laboured over the minute details of anatomy, piecing together sinews, veins, and muscles. The dissecting room and the slaughter-house furnished many of my materials, and often I shuddered at the very tasks I undertook.

Yet, as the days turned to weeks, and the weeks to months, I became blind to the horror of my work. The intricacies of my creation, the technical marvel of my progress, eclipsed the grim reality of what I was assembling.

Now, pacing my chamber on this night, those details came flooding back to me in vivid, nauseating clarity. The nights spent in graveyards, the hours bent over decaying remains—it all seemed a grotesque parody of creation.

> *Aside, Transition*
> *At length, exhaustion overtook me, and I threw myself onto my bed. But sleep brought no solace. Instead, it conjured horrors as vivid as the waking nightmare I had fled.*

I slept indeed, but I was disturbed by the wildest dreams. I thought I saw Elizabeth, in the bloom of health, walking in the streets of Ingolstadt. Delighted and surprised, I embraced her; but as I imprinted the first kiss on her lips, they became livid with the hue of death; her features appeared to change, and I thought that I held the corpse of my dead mother in my arms; a shroud enveloped her form, and I saw the grave-worms crawling in the folds of the flannel.

I started from my sleep with horror; a cold dew covered my forehead, my teeth chattered, and every limb became convulsed: when, by the dim and yellow light of the moon, as it forced its way through the window shutters, I beheld the wretch—the miserable monster whom I had created. He held up the curtain of the bed; and his eyes, if eyes they may be called, were fixed on me.

His jaws opened, and he muttered some inarticulate sounds, while a grin wrinkled his cheeks. He might have spoken, but I did not hear; one hand was stretched out, seemingly to detain me, but I escaped and rushed downstairs.

I took refuge in the courtyard belonging to the house which I inhabited; where I remained during the rest of the night, walking up and down in the greatest agitation, listening attentively, catching and fearing each sound as if it were to announce the approach of the demoniacal corpse to which I had so miserably given life.

Oh! No mortal could support the horror of that countenance. A mummy again endued with animation could not be so hideous as that wretch. I had gazed on him while unfinished; he was ugly then, but when those muscles and joints were rendered capable of motion, it became a thing such as even Dante could not have conceived.

I passed the night wretchedly. Sometimes my pulse beat so quickly and hardly that I felt the palpitation of every artery; at others, I nearly sank to the ground through languor and extreme weakness. Mingled with this horror, I felt the bitterness of disappointment; dreams that had been my food and pleasant rest for so long a space were now become a hell to me; and the change was so rapid, the overthrow so complete!

Morning, dismal and wet, at length dawned and I discovered to my sleepless and aching eyes the church of Ingolstadt, its white steeple and clock, which indicated the sixth hour. The porter opened the gates of the court, which had that night been my asylum, and I issued into the streets, pacing them with quick steps, as if I sought to avoid the wretch whom I feared every turning of the street would present to my view. I did not dare return to the apartment which I inhabited, but felt impelled to hurry on, although drenched by the rain which poured from a black and comfortless sky.

I continued walking in this manner for some time, endeavouring by bodily exercise to ease the load that weighed upon my mind. I traversed the streets without any clear conception of where I was or what I was doing. My heart palpitated in the sickness of fear, and I hurried on with irregular steps, not daring to look about me. I was reminded of the haunting lines from "The Rime of the Ancient Mariner", which captured my terror:

Like one who, on a lonely road,
Doth walk in fear and dread,
And, having once turned round, walks on,
And turns no more his head;
Because he knows a frightful fiend
Doth close behind him tread.

Closing Reflection
This night marked the beginning of a torment I could never escape. The creature I had abandoned would not remain silent or still, and its existence became a shadow over my every waking thought. My ambition had turned to ash, and in its place, I found only fear and regret.

15

A HAUNTED HOUSE

Virginia Woolf

WHATEVER HOUR you woke there was a door shutting. From room to room they went, hand in hand, lifting here, opening there, making sure—a ghostly couple.

"Here we left it," she said.

"Oh, but here too!" he added.

"It's upstairs," she murmured.

"And in the garden," he whispered.

"Quietly," they said, "or we shall wake them."

But it wasn't that you woke us. Oh, no. "They're looking for it; they're drawing the curtain," one might say, and so read on a page or two. "Now they've found it," one would be certain, stopping the pencil on the margin.

And then, tired of reading, one might rise and see for oneself, the house all empty, the doors standing open, only the wood pigeons bubbling with content and the hum of the threshing machine sounding from the farm.

"What did I come in here for? What did I want to find?" My hands were empty. "Perhaps it's upstairs then?" The apples were in the loft. And so down again, the garden still as ever, only the book had slipped into the grass.

But they had found it in the drawing room. Not that one could ever see them. The window panes reflected apples, reflected roses; all the leaves were green in the glass. If they moved in the drawing room, the apple only turned its yellow side. Yet, the moment after, if the door was opened, spread about the floor, hung upon the walls, pendant from the ceiling—what? My hands were empty.

The shadow of a thrush crossed the carpet; from the deepest wells of silence the wood pigeon drew its bubble of sound. "Safe, safe, safe," the pulse of the house beat softly. "The treasure buried; the room..." the pulse stopped short. Oh, was that the buried treasure?

A moment later the light had faded. Out in the garden then? But the trees spun darkness for a wandering beam of sun. So fine, so rare, coolly sunk beneath the surface the beam I sought always burnt behind the glass. Death was the glass; death was between us; coming to the woman first, hundreds of years ago, leaving the house, sealing all the windows; the rooms were darkened. He left it, left her, went North, went East, saw the stars turned in the Southern sky; sought the house, found it dropped beneath the Downs. "Safe, safe, safe," the pulse of the house beat gladly. "The Treasure yours."

The wind roars up the avenue. Trees stoop and bend this way and that. Moonbeams splash and spill wildly in the rain. But the beam of the lamp falls straight from the window. The candle burns stiff and still. Wandering through the house, opening the windows, whispering not to wake us, the ghostly couple seek their joy.

"Here we slept," she says.

And he adds, "Kisses without number."

"Waking in the morning—"

"Silver between the trees —"

"Upstairs—"

"In the garden—"

"When summer came—"

"In winter snowtime—"

The doors go shutting far in the distance, gently knocking like the pulse of a heart.

Nearer they come; cease at the doorway. The wind falls, the rain slides silver down the glass. Our eyes darken; we hear no steps beside us; we see no lady spread her ghostly cloak. His hands shield the lantern.

"Look," he breathes. "Sound asleep. Love upon their lips."

Stooping, holding their silver lamp above us, long they look and deeply. Long they pause. The wind drives straightly; the flame stoops slightly. Wild beams of moonlight cross both floor and wall, and, meeting, stain the faces bent; the faces pondering; the faces that search the sleepers and seek their hidden joy.

"Safe, safe, safe," the heart of the house beats proudly.

"Long years—" he sighs.

"Again you found me."

"Here," she murmurs, "sleeping; in the garden reading; laughing, rolling apples in the loft. Here we left our treasure—" Stooping, their light lifts the lids upon my eyes.

"Safe! safe! safe!" the pulse of the house beats wildly. Waking, I cry "Oh, is this your buried treasure? The light in the heart."

15

IN A GROVE

Ryūnosuke Akutagawa

The Testimony of a Woodcutter
Questioned by a High Police Commissioner

Yes, sir. Certainly, it was I who found the body. This morning, as usual, I went to cut my daily quota of cedars when I found the body in a grove, in a hollow in the mountains. The exact location? About 150 meters off the Yamashina stage road. It's an out-of-the-way grove of bamboo and cedars.

The body was lying flat on its back dressed in a bluish silk kimono and a wrinkled headdress of the Kyoto style. A single sword-stroke had pierced the breast. The fallen bamboo blades around it were stained with bloody blossoms. No, the blood was no longer running. The wound had dried up, I believe. And also, a gadfly was stuck fast there, hardly noticing my footsteps.

You ask me if I saw a sword or any such thing?

No, nothing, sir. I found only a rope at the root of a cedar nearby. And... well, in addition to a rope, I found a comb. That was all. Apparently he must have made a battle of it before he was murdered, because the grass and fallen bamboo blades had been trampled down all around.

"A horse was near by?"

No, sir. It's hard enough for a man to enter, let alone a horse.

The Testimony of a Traveling Buddhist Priest
Questioned by a High Police Commissioner

The time? Certainly, it was about noon yesterday, sir. The unfortunate man was on the road from Sekiyama to Yamashina. He was walking toward Sekiyama with a woman accompanying him on horseback, whom I have since learned was his wife. A scarf hanging from her head hid her face from view. All I saw was the colour of her clothes, a lilac-coloured suit. Her horse was a sorrel with a fine mane. The lady's height? Oh, about four feet five inches. Since I am a Buddhist priest, I took little notice about her details. Well, the man was armed with a sword as well as a bow and arrows. And I remember that he carried some 20-odd arrows in his quiver.

Little did I expect that he would meet such a fate. Truly human life is as evanescent as the morning dew or a flash of lightning. My words are inadequate to express my sympathy for him.

The Testimony of a Policeman
Questioned by a High Police Commissioner

The man that I arrested? He is a notorious brigand called Tajomaru. When I arrested him, he had fallen off his horse.

He was groaning on the bridge at Awataguchi. The time? It was in the early hours of last night. For the record, I might say that the other day I tried to arrest him, but unfortunately he escaped. He was wearing a dark blue silk kimono and a large plain sword. And, as you see, he had gotten a bow and arrows somewhere. You say that this bow and these arrows look like the ones owned by the dead man? Then Tajomaru must be the murderer. The bow wound with leather strips, the black lacquered quiver, the seventeen arrows with hawk feathers—these were all in his possession, I believe. Yes, sir, the horse is, as you say, a sorrel with a fine mane. A little beyond the stone bridge, I found the horse grazing by the roadside, with his long rein dangling. Surely there is some providence in his having been thrown by the horse.

Of all the robbers prowling around Kyoto, this Tajomaru has given the most grief to the women in town. Last autumn a wife who came to the mountain back of the Pindora of the Toribe Temple, presumably to pay a visit, was murdered, along with a girl. It has been suspected that it was his doing. If this criminal murdered the man, you cannot tell what he may have done with the man's wife. May it please your honour to look into this problem as well.

The Testimony of an Old Woman

Questioned by a High Police Commissioner

Yes, sir, that corpse is the man who married my daughter. He does not come from Kyoto. He was a samurai in the town of Kokufu in the province of Wakasa. His name was Kanazawa no Takehiko, and his age was twenty-six. He was of a gentle disposition, so I am sure he did nothing to provoke the anger of others.

My daughter? Her name is Masago, and her age is nineteen. She is a spirited, fun-loving girl, but I am sure she has never known any man except Takehiko. She has a small, oval, dark-complected face with a mole at the corner of her left eye.

Yesterday Takehiko left for Wakasa with my daughter. What bad luck it is that things should have come to such a sad end! What has become of my daughter? I am resigned to giving up my son-in-law as lost, but the fate of my daughter worries me sick. For Heaven's sake leave no stone unturned to find her. I hate that robber Tajomaru, or whatever his name is. Not only my son-in-law, but my daughter ... (Her later words were drowned in tears.)

Tajomaru's Confession

I killed him, but not her. Where's she gone? I can't tell. Oh, wait a minute. No torture can make me confess what I don't know. Now things have come to such a head, I won't keep anything from you.

Yesterday a little past noon I met that couple. Just then, a puff of wind blew and raised her hanging scarf, so that I caught a glimpse of her face. Instantly it was again covered from my view. That may have been one reason—she looked like a Bodhisattva. At that moment I made up my mind to capture her even if I had to kill her man.

Why? To me killing isn't a matter of such great consequence as you might think. When a woman is captured, her man has to be killed anyway. In killing, I use the sword I wear at my side. Am I the only one who kills people? You, you don't use your swords. You kill people with your power, with your money. Sometimes you kill them on the pretext of working for their good. It's true they don't bleed. They are in the best of health, but all the same you've killed them. It's hard to say who is a greater sinner, you or me.

But it would be good if I could capture a woman without killing her man. So, I made up my mind to capture her and do my best not to kill him. But it's out of the question on the Yamashina stage road. So I managed to lure the couple into the mountains.

It was quite easy. I became their travelling companion, and I told them there was an old mound in the mountain over there, and that I had dug it open and found many mirrors and swords. I went on to tell them I'd buried the things in a grove behind the mountain, and that I'd like to sell them at a low price to anyone who would care to have them. Then ... you see, isn't greed terrible? He was beginning to be moved by my talk before he knew it. In less than half an hour they were driving their horse toward the mountain with me.

When he came in front of the grove, I told them that the treasures were buried in it, and I asked them to come and see. The man had no objection— he was blinded by greed. The woman said she would wait on horseback. It was natural for her to say so, at the sight of a thick grove. To tell you the truth, my plan worked just as I wished, so I went into the grove with him, leaving her behind alone.

The grove is only bamboo for some distance. About fifty yards ahead there's a rather open clump of cedars. It was a convenient spot for my purpose. Pushing my way through the grove, I told him a plausible lie that the treasures were buried under the cedars. When I told him this, he pushed his laborious way toward the slender cedar visible through the grove. After a while the bamboo thinned out, and we came to where a number of cedars grew in a row. As soon as we got there, I seized him from behind. Because he was a trained, sword-bearing warrior, he was quite strong, but he was taken by surprise, so there was no help for him. I soon tied him up to the root of a cedar. Where did I get a rope? Thank heaven, being a robber, I had a rope with me, since I might have to scale a wall at any moment. Of course, it was easy to stop him from calling out by gagging his mouth with fallen bamboo leaves.

When I disposed of him, I went to his woman and asked her to come and see him, because he seemed to have been suddenly taken sick. It's needless to say that this plan also worked well. The woman, her sedge hat off, came into the depths of the grove, where I led her by the hand. The instant she caught sight of her husband, she drew a small sword.

I've never seen a woman of such violent temper. If I'd been off guard, I'd have got a thrust in my side. I dodged, but she kept on slashing at me. She might have wounded me deeply or killed me. But I'm Tajomaru. I managed to strike down her small sword without drawing my own. The most spirited woman is defenceless without a weapon. At least I could satisfy my desire for her without taking her husband's life.

Yes ... without taking his life. I had no wish to kill him. I was about to run away from the grove, leaving the woman behind in tears, when she frantically clung to my arm. In broken fragments of words, she asked that either her husband or I die. She said it was more trying than death to have her shame known to two men. She gasped out that she wanted to be the wife of whichever survived. Then a furious desire to kill him seized me.

Telling you in this way, no doubt I seem a crueller man than you. But that's because you didn't see her face. Especially her burning eyes at that moment. As I saw her eye to eye, I wanted to make her my wife even if I were to be struck by lightning. I wanted to make her my wife ... this single desire filled my mind. This was not only lust, as you might think. At that time if I'd had no other desire than lust, I'd surely not have minded knocking her down and running away. Then I wouldn't have stained my sword with his blood. But the moment I gazed at her face in the dark grove, I decided not to leave there without killing him.

But I didn't like to resort to unfair means to kill him. I untied him and told him to cross swords with me. (The rope that was found at the root of the cedar is the rope I dropped at the time.) Furious with anger, he drew his thick sword. And quick as thought, he sprang at me ferociously, without speaking a word. I needn't tell you how our fight turned out. The twenty-third stroke... please remember this. I'm impressed with this fact still. Nobody under the sun has ever clashed swords with me for twenty strokes. When he fell, I turned toward her, lowering my blood-stained sword. But to my great astonishment she was gone. I wondered where she had run away. I looked for her in the clump of cedars. I listened, but heard only a groaning sound from the throat of the dying man.

As soon as we started to cross swords, she may have run away through the grove to call for help. When I thought of that, I decided it was a matter of life and death to me. So, robbing him of his sword and bow and arrows, I ran out to the mountain road. There I found her horse still grazing quietly. It would be a mere waste of words to tell you the later details, but before I entered town I had already parted with the sword. That's all my confession. I know that my head will be hung in chains anyway, so put me down for the maximum penalty.

The Repentance of a Woman

Who Has Come to Kiyomizu Temple

That man in the blue silk kimono, after forcing me to yield to him, laughed mockingly as he looked at my bound husband. How horrified my husband must have been! But no matter how hard he struggled in agony, the rope cut into him all the more tightly. In spite of myself I ran stumblingly toward his side. Or rather I tried to run toward him, but the man instantly knocked me down. Just at that moment I saw an indescribable light in my husband's eyes. Something beyond expression ... his eyes make me shudder even now. That instantaneous look of my husband, who couldn't speak a word, told me all his heart. The flash in his eyes was neither anger nor sorrow ... only a cold light, a look of loathing. More struck by the look in his eyes than by the blow of the thief, I called out in spite of myself and fell unconscious.

In the course of time I came to, and found that the man in blue silk was gone. I saw only my husband still bound to the root of the cedar. I raised myself from the bamboo blades with difficulty, and looked into his face; but the expression in his eyes was just the same as before.

Beneath the cold contempt in his eyes, there was hatred. Shame, grief, and anger ... I don't know how to express my heart at that time. Reeling to my feet, I went up to my husband.

"Takejiro," I said to him, "since things have come to this pass, I cannot live with you. I'm determined to die ... but you must die, too. You saw my shame. I can't leave you alive as you are." This was all I could say. Still he went on gazing at me with loathing and contempt. My heart breaking, I looked for his sword. It must have been taken by the robber. Neither his sword nor his bow and arrows were to be seen in the grove. But fortunately my small sword was lying at my feet. Raising it overhead, once more I said, "Now give me your life. I'll follow you right away."

When he heard these words, he moved his lips with difficulty. Since his mouth was stuffed with leaves, of course his voice could not be heard at all. But at a glance I understood his words. Despising me, his look said only, "Kill me." Neither conscious nor unconscious, I stabbed the small sword through the lilac-coloured kimono into his breast.

Again at this time I must have fainted. By the time I managed to look up, he had already breathed his last—still in bonds. A streak of sinking sunlight streamed through the clump of cedars and bamboos, and shone on his pale face. Gulping down my sobs, I untied the rope from his dead body. And... and what has become of me? Only that, since I have no more strength to tell you. Anyway, I hadn't the strength to die. I stabbed my own throat with the small sword, I threw myself into a pond at the foot of the mountain, and I tried to kill myself in many ways. Unable to end my life, I am still living in dishonour. Worthless as I am, I must have been forsaken even by the most merciful Kwannon. I killed my own husband. I was violated by the robber. Whatever can I do? Whatever can I ... I ...

The Story of the Murdered Man,
As Told Through a Medium

After violating my wife, the robber, sitting there, began to speak comforting words to her. Of course I couldn't speak. My whole body was tied fast to the root of a cedar. But meanwhile I winked at her many times, as much as to say "Don't believe the robber." I wanted to convey some such meaning to her. But my wife, sitting dejectedly on the bamboo leaves, was looking hard at her lap. To all appearance, she was listening to his words. I was agonized by jealousy. In the meantime the robber went on with his clever talk, from one subject to another. The robber finally made his bold brazen proposal. "Once your virtue is stained, you won't get along well with your husband, so won't you be my wife instead? It's my love for you that made me be violent toward you."

While the criminal talked, my wife raised her face as if in a trance. She had never looked so beautiful as at that moment. What did my beautiful wife say in answer to him while I was sitting bound there? I am lost in space, but I have never thought of her answer without burning with anger and jealousy. Truly she said, … "Then take me away with you wherever you go."

This is not the whole of her sin. If that were all, I would not be tormented so much in the dark. When she was going out of the grove as if in a dream, her hand in the robber's, she suddenly turned pale, and pointed at me tied to the root of the cedar, and said, "Kill him! I cannot marry you as long as he lives." "Kill him!" she cried many times, as if she had gone crazy. Even now these words threaten to blow me headlong into the bottomless abyss of darkness.

Has such a hateful thing come out of a human mouth ever before? Have such cursed words ever struck a human ear, even once? Even once such a …

At these words the robber himself turned pale. "Kill him," she cried, clinging to his arms. Looking hard at her, he answered neither yes nor no … but hardly had I thought about his answer before she had been knocked down into the bamboo leaves. (Again a cry of scorn.) Quietly folding his arms, he looked at me and said, "What will you do with her?

Kill her or save her? You have only to nod. Kill her?" For these words alone I would like to pardon his crime.

While I hesitated, she shrieked and ran into the depths of the grove. The robber instantly snatched at her, but he failed even to grasp her sleeve.

After she ran away, he took up my sword, and my bow and arrows. With a single stroke he cut one of my bonds. I remember his mumbling, "My fate is next." Then he disappeared from the grove. All was silent after that. No, I heard someone crying. Untying the rest of my bonds, I listened carefully, and I noticed that it was my own crying.

I raised my exhausted body from the foot of the cedar. In front of me there was shining the small sword which my wife had dropped. I took it up and stabbed it into my breast. A bloody lump rose to my mouth, but I didn't feel any pain. When my breast grew cold, everything was as silent as the dead in their graves. What profound silence! Not a single bird note was heard in the sky over this grave in the hollow of the mountains. Only a lonely light lingered on the cedars and mountains. By and by the light gradually grew fainter, till the cedars and bamboo were lost to view. Lying there, I was enveloped in deep silence.

Then someone crept up to me. I tried to see who it was. But darkness had already been gathering round me. Someone ... that someone drew the small sword softly out of my breast in its invisible hand. At the same time once more blood flowed into my mouth. And once and for all I sank down into the darkness of space.

15

A VISION OF HORROR

Helena Blavatsky

HOW STRANGE! Where was I? It was evident to me that I had once more returned to my senses. For there I was, vividly realizing that I was rapidly moving forward, while experiencing a queer, strange sensation as though I were swimming, without impulse or effort on my part, and in total darkness. The idea that first presented itself to me was that of a long subterranean passage of water, of earth, and stifling air, though bodily I had no perception, no sensation, of the presence or contact of any of these. I tried to utter a few words, to repeat my last sentence, "I desire but one thing: to learn the reason or reasons why my sister has so suddenly ceased writing to me,"—but the only words I heard out of the twenty-one, were the two, "to learn," and these, instead of their coming out of my own larynx, came back to me in my own voice, but entirely outside myself, near, but not in me. In short, they were pronounced by my voice, not by my lips.

One more rapid, involuntary motion, one more plunge into the Cimmerian darkness of a (to me) unknown element, and I saw myself standing—actually standing underground, as it seemed. I was compactly and thickly surrounded on all sides, above and below, right and left, with earth, and in the mould, and yet it weighed not, and seemed quite immaterial and transparent to my senses. I did not realize for one second the utter absurdity, nay, the impossibility of that seeming fact! One second more, one short instant, and I perceived—oh, inexpressible horror when I think of it now—for then, although I perceived, realized, and recorded facts and events far more clearly than ever I had done before, I did not seem to be touched in any other way by what I saw.

Yes, I perceived a coffin at my feet. It was a plain, unpretentious shell, made of deal, the last couch of the pauper, in which, notwithstanding its closed lid—I plainly saw a hideous, grinning skull, a man's skeleton, mutilated and broken in many of its parts, as though it had been taken out of some hidden chamber of the defunct Inquisition, where it had been subjected to torture. "Who can it be?" I thought.

At this moment I heard again proceeding from afar the same voice—my voice... "the reason or reasons why"... it said; as though these words were the unbroken continuation of the same sentence of which it had just repeated the two words "to learn." It sounded near, and yet as from some incalculable distance; giving me then the idea that the long subterranean journey, the subsequent mental reflexions and discoveries, had occupied no time; had been performed during the short, almost instantaneous interval between the first and the middle words of the sentence, begun, at any rate, if not actually pronounced by myself in my room at Kioto, and which it was now finishing, in interrupted, broken phrases, like a faithful echo of my own words and voice...

Forthwith, the hideous, mangled remains began assuming a form, and, to me, but too familiar appearance. The broken parts joined together one to the other, the bones became covered once more with flesh, and I recognized in these disfigured remains—with some surprise, but not a trace of feeling at the sight—my sister's dead husband, my own brother-in-law, whom I had for her sake loved so truly. *How was it, and how did he come to die such a terrible death?* I asked myself. To put oneself a query seemed, in the state in which I was, to instantly solve it. Hardly had I asked myself the question, when as if in a panorama, I saw the retrospective picture of poor Karl's death, in all its horrid vividness, and with every thrilling detail, every one of which, however, left me then entirely and brutally indifferent. Here he is, the dear old fellow, full of life and joy at the prospect of more lucrative employment from his principal, examining and trying in a wood-sawing factory a monster steam engine just arrived from America. He bends over, to examine more closely an inner arrangement, to tighten a screw. His clothes are caught by the teeth of the revolving wheel in full motion, and suddenly he is dragged down, doubled up, and his limbs half-severed, torn off, before the workmen, unacquainted with the mechanism, can stop it.

He is taken out, or what remains of him, dead, mangled, a thing of horror, an unrecognizable mass of palpitating flesh and blood! I follow the remains, wheeled as an unrecognizable heap to the hospital, hear the brutally given order that the messengers of death should stop on their way at the house of the widow and orphans. I follow them, and find the unconscious family quietly assembled together. I see my sister, the dear and beloved, and remain indifferent at the sight, only feeling highly interested in the coming scene. My heart, my feelings, even my personality, seemed to have disappeared, to have been left behind, to belong to somebody else.

There "I" stand, and witness her unprepared reception of the ghastly news. I realize clearly, without one moment's hesitation or mistake, the effect of the shock upon her, I perceived clearly, following and recording, to the minutest detail, her sensations and the inner process that takes place in her. I watch and remember, missing not one single point.

As the corpse is brought into the house for identification I hear the long agonizing cry, my own name pronounced, and the dull thud of the living body falling upon the remains of the dead one. I followed with curiosity the sudden thrill and the instantaneous perturbation in her brain that follow it, and watch with attention the worm-like, precipitate, and immensely intensified motion of the tubular fibres, the instantaneous change of colour in the cephalic extremity of the nervous system, the fibrous nervous matter passing from white to bright red and then to a dark red, bluish hue.

I notice the sudden flash of a phosphorous-like, brilliant Radiance, its tremor and its sudden extinction followed by darkness—complete darkness in the region of memory—as the Radiance, comparable in its form only to a human shape, oozes out suddenly from the top of the head, expands, loses its form and scatters. And I say to myself: *This is insanity; lifelong, incurable insanity, for the principle of intelligence is not paralyzed or extinguished temporarily, but has just deserted the tabernacle forever, ejected from it by the terrible force of the sudden blow.... The link between the animal and the divine essence is broken.* And as the unfamiliar term "divine" is mentally uttered, my "thought" laughs.

Suddenly, I hear again my far-off, yet-near voice pronouncing emphatically and close by me the words... "why my sister has so suddenly ceased writing." And before the two final words "to me" have completed the sentence, I see a long series of sad events, immediately following the catastrophe.

I behold the mother, now a helpless, grovelling idiot, in the lunatic asylum attached to the city hospital, the seven younger children admitted into a refuge for paupers. Finally I see the two elder, a boy of fifteen and a girl a year younger, my favourites, both taken by strangers into their service. A captain of a sailing vessel carries away my nephew, an old Jewess adopts the tender girl. I see the events with all their horrors and thrilling details, and record each, to the smallest detail, with the utmost coolness.

For, mark well: when I use such expressions as horrors etc., they are to be understood as an afterthought. During the whole time of the events described I experienced no sensation of either pain or pity. My feelings seemed to be paralyzed as well as my external senses; it was only after "coming back" that I realized my irretrievable losses to their full extent.

Much of that which I had so vehemently denied in those days, owing to sad personal experience, I have to admit now. Had I been told by any one at that time, that man could act and think and feel, irrespective of his brain and senses; nay, that by some mysterious, and to this day, for me, incomprehensible power, he could be transported mentally, thousands of miles away from his body, there to witness not only present but also past events, and remember these by storing them in his memory—I would have proclaimed that man as a madman. Alas, I can do so no longer, for I have become myself that "madman." Ten, twenty, forty, a hundred times during the course of this wretched life of mine, have I experienced and lived over such moments of existence, outside of my body. Accursed be that hour when this terrible power was first awakened in me! I have not even the consolation left of attributing such glimpses of events at a distance to insanity. Madmen rave and see that which exists not in the realm they belong to. My visions have proved invariably correct. But to my narrative of woe.

I had hardly had time to see my unfortunate young niece in her new Israelitish home, when I felt a shock of the same nature as the one that had sent me "swimming" through the bowels of the earth, as I had thought. I opened my eyes in my own room, and the first thing I fixed upon, by accident, was the clock. The hands of the dial showed seven minutes and a half past five!... I had thus passed through these most terrible experiences which it takes me hours to narrate, in precisely half a minute of time!

But this, too, was an afterthought. For one brief instant I recollected nothing of what I had seen. Uttering a cry of horror and despair, I felt as though the whole creation were crushing me under its weight. For one moment I remained speechless, the picture of human ruin amid a world of death and desolation. My heart sank down in anguish: my doom was closed; and a hopeless gloom seemed to settle over the rest of my life, forever.

19

A GHOST STORY

Mark Twain

I TOOK a large room, far up Broadway, in a huge old building whose upper stories had been wholly unoccupied for years, until I came. The place had long been given up to dust and cobwebs, to solitude and silence. I seemed groping among the tombs and invading the privacy of the dead, that first night I climbed up to my quarters. For the first time in my life a superstitious dread came over me, and as I turned a dark angle of the stairway and an invisible cobweb swung its lazy woof in my face and clung there, I shuddered as one who had encountered a phantom.

I was glad enough when I reached my room and locked out the mould and the darkness. A cheery fire was burning in the grate, and I sat down before it with a comforting sense of relief. For two hours I sat there, thinking of bygone times;

recalling old scenes, and summoning half-forgotten faces out of the mists of the past; listening, in fancy, to voices that long ago grew silent for all time, and to once familiar songs that nobody sings now, and as my reverie softened down to a sadder and sadder pathos, the shrieking of the winds outside softened to a wail, the angry beating of the rain against the panes diminished to a tranquil patter, and one by one the noises in the street subsided, until the hurrying footsteps of the last belated straggler died away in the distance and left no sound behind.

The fire had burned low. A sense of loneliness crept over me. I arose and undressed, moving on tiptoe about the room, doing stealthily what I had to do, as if I were environed by sleeping enemies whose slumbers it would be fatal to break. I covered up in bed, and lay listening to the rain and wind and the faint creaking of distant shutters, till they lulled me to sleep.

I slept profoundly, but how long I do not know. All at once I found myself awake, and filled with a shuddering expectancy. All was still. All but my own heart—I could hear it beat. Presently the bedclothes began to slip away slowly toward the foot of the bed, as if some one were pulling them! I could not stir; I could not speak. Still the blankets slipped deliberately away, till my breast was uncovered. Then with a great effort I seized them and drew them over my head. I waited, listened, waited.

Once more that steady pull began, and once more I lay torpid for a century of dragging seconds till my breast was naked again. At last I roused my energies and snatched the covers back to their place and held them with a strong grip. I waited. By and by I felt a faint tug, and took a fresh grip. The tug strengthened to a steady strain—it grew stronger and stronger. My hold parted, and for the third time the blankets slid away. I groaned. An answering groan came from the foot of the bed! Beaded drops of sweat stood upon my forehead. I was more dead than alive. Presently I heard a heavy footstep in my room—the step of an elephant, it seemed to me—it was not like anything human. But it was moving from me—there was relief in that. I heard it approach the door—pass out without moving bolt or lock—and wander away among the dismal corridors, straining the floors and joists till they creaked again as it passed—and then silence reigned once more.

When my excitement had calmed, I said to myself, "This is a dream—simply a hideous dream." And so I lay thinking it over until I convinced myself that it was a dream, and then a comforting laugh relaxed my lips and I was happy again. I got up and struck a light, and when I found that the locks and bolts were just as I had left them, another soothing laugh welled in my heart and rippled from my lips.

I took my pipe and lit it, and was just sitting down before the fire, when—down went the pipe out of my nerveless fingers, the blood forsook my cheeks, and my placid breathing was cut short with a gasp! In the ashes on the hearth, side by side with my own bare footprint, was another, so vast that in comparison mine was but an infant's! Then I had a visitor, and the elephant tread was explained.

I put out the light and returned to bed, palsied with fear. I lay a long time, peering into the darkness, and listening. Then I heard a grating noise overhead, like the dragging of a heavy body across the floor; then the throwing down of the body, and the shaking of my windows in response to the concussion. In distant parts of the building, I heard the muffled slamming of doors. I heard, at intervals, stealthy footsteps creeping in and out among the corridors, and up and down the stairs. Sometimes these noises approached my door, hesitated, and went away again. I heard the clanking of chains faintly, in remote passages, and listened while the clanking grew nearer—while it wearily climbed the stairways, marking each move by the loose surplus of chain that fell with an accented rattle upon each succeeding step as the goblin that bore it advanced. I heard muttered sentences; half-uttered screams that seemed smothered violently; and the swish of invisible garments, the rush of invisible wings.

Then I became conscious that my chamber was invaded—that I was not alone. I heard sighs and breathings about my bed, and mysterious whisperings. Three little spheres of soft phosphorescent light appeared on the ceiling directly over my head, clung and glowed there a moment, then dropped—two of them upon my face and one upon the pillow. They spattered, liquidly, and felt warm. Intuition told me they had turned to gouts of blood as they fell—I needed no light to satisfy myself of that.

Then I saw pallid faces, dimly luminous, and white uplifted hands, floating bodiless in the air—floating a moment and then disappearing. The whispering ceased, the voices and the sounds, and a solemn stillness followed. I waited and listened. I felt that I must have light or die. I was weak with fear. I slowly raised myself toward a sitting posture, and my face came in contact with a clammy hand! All strength went from me apparently, and I fell back like a stricken invalid. Then I heard the rustle of a garment—it seemed to pass to the door and go out.

When everything was still once more, I crept out of bed, sick and feeble, and lit the gas with a hand that trembled as if it were aged with a hundred years. The light brought some little cheer to my spirits. I sat down and fell into a dreamy contemplation of that great footprint in the ashes. By and by its outlines began to waver and grow dim. I glanced up and the broad gas flame was slowly wilting away. In the same moment I heard that elephantine tread again. I noted its approach, nearer and nearer, along the musty halls, and dimmer and dimmer the light waned.

The tread reached my very door and paused—the light had dwindled to a sickly blue, and all things about me lay in a spectral twilight. The door did not open, and yet I felt a faint gust of air fan my cheek, and presently was conscious of a huge, cloudy presence before me. I watched it with fascinated eyes. A pale glow stole over the Thing; gradually its cloudy folds took shape—an arm appeared, then legs, then a body, and last a great sad face looked out of the vapor. Stripped of its filmy housings—naked, muscular and comely, the majestic Cardiff Giant loomed above me!

All my misery vanished—for a child might know that no harm could come with that benignant countenance. My cheerful spirits returned at once, and in sympathy with them the gas flamed up brightly again. Never a lonely outcast was so glad to welcome company as I was to greet the friendly giant. I said:

"Why, is it nobody but you? Do you know, I have been scared to death for the last two or three hours? I am most honestly glad to see you. I wish I had a chair—Here, here, don't try to sit down in that thing!" But it was too late. He was in it before I could stop him, and down he went—I never saw a chair shivered so in my life.

"Stop, stop, you'll ruin ev—"

Too late again. There was another crash, and another chair was resolved into its original elements.

"Confound it, haven't you got any judgment at all? Do you want to ruin all the furniture on the place? Here, here, you petrified fool—" But it was no use. Before I could arrest him, he had sat down on the bed, and it was a melancholy ruin.

"Now what sort of a way is that to do? First you come lumbering about the place bringing a legion of vagabond goblins along with you to worry me to death, and then when I overlook an indelicacy of costume which would not be tolerated anywhere by cultivated people except in a respectable theater, and not even there if the nudity were of your sex, you repay me by wrecking all the furniture you can find to sit down on. And why will you? You damage yourself as much as you do me. You have broken off the end of your spinal column, and littered up the floor with chips of your hams till the place looks like a marble yard. You ought to be ashamed of yourself—you are big enough to know better."

"Well, I will not break any more furniture. But what am I to do? I have not had a chance to sit down for a century." And the tears came into his eyes.

"Poor devil," I said, "I should not have been so harsh with you. And you are an orphan, too, no doubt. But sit down on the floor here—nothing else can stand your weight, and besides, we cannot be sociable with you away up there above me; I want you down where I can perch on this high counting-house stool and gossip with you face to face."

So he sat down on the floor, and lit a pipe which I gave him, threw one of my red blankets over his shoulders, inverted my sitz-bath on his head, helmet fashion, and made himself picturesque and comfortable. Then he crossed his ankles, while I renewed the fire, and exposed the flat, honeycombed bottoms of his prodigious feet to the grateful warmth.

"What is the matter with the bottom of your feet and the back of your legs, that they are gouged up so?"

"Infernal chilblains—I caught them clear up to the back of my head, roosting out there under Newell's farm. But I love the place; I love it as one loves his old home. There is no peace for me like the peace I feel when I am there."

We talked along for half an hour, and then I noticed that

he looked tired, and spoke of it. "Tired?" he said. "Well, I should think so, and now I will tell you all about it, since you have treated me so well. I am the spirit of the Petrified Man that lies across the street there in the Museum. I am the ghost of the Cardiff Giant.

I can have no rest, no peace, till they have given that poor body burial again. Now what was the most natural thing for me to do, to make men satisfy this wish? Terrify them into it!—haunt the place where the body lay! So I haunted the museum night after night. I even got other spirits to help me. But it did no good, for nobody ever came to the museum at midnight.

Then it occurred to me to come over the way and haunt this place a little. I felt that if I ever got a hearing I must succeed, for I had the most efficient company that perdition could furnish. Night after night we have shivered around through these mildewed halls, dragging chains, groaning, whispering, tramping up and down stairs, till, to tell you the truth, I am almost worn out. But when I saw a light in your room to-night I roused my energies again and went at it with a deal of the old freshness. But I am tired out—entirely fagged out. Give me, I beseech you, give me some hope!"

I lit off my perch in a burst of excitement, and exclaimed:

"This transcends everything—everything that ever did occur! Why you poor blundering old fossil, you have had all your trouble for nothing—you have been haunting a plaster cast of yourself—the real Cardiff Giant is in Albany!

"Confound it, don't you know your own remains?"

I never saw such an eloquent look of shame, of pitiable humiliation, overspread a countenance before. The Petrified Man rose slowly to his feet, and said:

"Honestly, is that true?"

"As true as I am sitting here."

He took the pipe from his mouth and laid it on the

mantel, then stood irresolute a moment (unconsciously, from old habit, thrusting his hands where his pantaloons pockets should have been, and meditatively dropping his chin on his breast), and finally said:

"Well—I never felt so absurd before. The Petrified Man has sold everybody else, and now the mean fraud has ended by selling its own ghost! My son, if there is any charity left in your heart for a poor friendless phantom like me, don't let this get out. Think how you would feel if you had made such an ass of yourself."

I heard his stately tramp die away, step by step down the stairs and out into the deserted street, and felt sorry that he was gone, poor fellow—and sorrier still that he had carried off my red blanket and my bathtub.

19

EYES OF THE PANTHER

Ambrose Bierce

A MAN AND A WOMAN, nature had done the grouping, sat on a rustic seat, in the late afternoon. The man was middle-aged, slender, swarthy, with the expression of a poet and the complexion of a pirate—a man at whom one would look again. The woman was young, raven-haired, graceful, with something in her figure and movements suggesting the word "lithe." She was habited in a grey gown with odd brown markings in the texture. She may have been beautiful; one could not readily say, for her eyes denied attention to all else. They were grey-green, long and narrow, with an expression defying analysis. One could only know that they were disquieting. Cleopatra may have had such eyes.

The man and the woman talked.

"Yes," said the woman, "I love you, God knows! But marry you? No. I cannot, will not."

"Irene, you have said that many times, yet always have denied me a reason. I've a right to know, to understand, to feel and prove my fortitude if I have it. Give me a reason."

"For loving you?" The woman was smiling through her tears and her pallor. That did not stir any sense of humour in the man.

''No. There is no reason for that. A reason for not marrying me. I've a right to know. I must know. I will know!"

He had risen and was standing before her with clenched hands, on his face a frown—it might have been called a scowl. He looked as if he might attempt to learn by strangling her. She smiled no more, merely sat looking up into his face with a fixed, set regard that was utterly without emotion or sentiment. Yet it had something in it that tamed his resentment and made him shiver.

"You are determined to have my reason?" she asked in a tone that was entirely mechanical, a tone that might have been her look, made audible.

"If you please, if I'm not asking too much." Apparently this lord of creation was yielding some part of his dominion over his co creature.

"Very well, you shall know: I am insane."

The man started, then looked incredulous and was conscious that he ought to be amused.

But, again, the sense of humour failed him in his need and despite his disbelief he was profoundly disturbed by that which he did not believe. Between our convictions and our feelings there is no good understanding.

"That is what the physicians would say," the woman continued. "I might myself prefer to call it a case of 'possession.' Sit down and hear what I have to say."

The man silently resumed his seat beside her on the rustic bench by the wayside. Over against them on the eastern side of the valley, the hills were already sun-set-flushed and the stillness all about was of that peculiar quality that foretells the twilight. Something of its mysterious and significant solemnity had imparted itself to the man's mood. In the spiritual, as in the material world, are signs and presages of night.

Rarely meeting her look, and whenever he did so, conscious of the indefinable dread with which, despite their feline beauty, her eyes always affected him, Jenner Brading listened in silence to the story told by Irene Marlowe. In deference to the reader's possible prejudice against the artless method of an unpractised historian, the author ventures to substitute his own version for hers.

In a little log house containing a single room sparely and rudely furnished, crouching on the floor against one of the walls was a woman, clasping to her breast a child. Outside, a dense unbroken forest extended for many miles in every direction. This was at night and the room was black-dark: no human eye could have discerned the woman and the child. Yet they were observed, narrowly, vigilantly, with never even a momentary slackening of attention; and that is the pivotal fact upon which this narrative turns.

Charles Marlowe was of the class, now cxtinct in this country, of woodmen pioneers—men who found their most acceptable surroundings in sylvan solitudes that stretched along the eastern slope of the Mississippi Valley, from the Great Lakes to the Gulf of Mexico. For more than a hundred years these men pushed ever westward, generation after generation, with rifle and axe, reclaiming from Nature and her savage children here and there an isolated acreage for the plow, no sooner reclaimed than surrendered to their less-venturesome but more-thrifty successors. At last they burst through the edge of the forest into the open country and vanished as if they had fallen over a cliff. The woodman pioneer is no more; the "pioneer of the plains"—he whose easy task it is to subdue for occupancy two-thirds of the country in a single generation—is another and inferior creation.

With Charles Marlowe in the wilderness, sharing the dangers and hardships of that strange, unprofitable life, were his wife and child, to whom, in the manner of his class in which the domestic virtues were a religion, he was passionately attached. The woman was still young enough to be comely, new enough to the awful isolation of her lot to be cheerful. By withholding the large capacity for happiness, which the simple satisfactions of the forest life could not have filled, Heaven had dealt honourably with her. In her household tasks, her child, her husband, and her few foolish books, she found abundant provision for her needs.

One morning in midsummer Marlowe took down his rifle from the wooden hooks on the wall and signified his intention of getting game.

"We've meat enough," said the wife. "Please don't go out today. I dreamed last night, oh, such a dreadful thing! I cannot recollect it, but I'm almost sure that it will come to pass if you go out."

It is painful to confess that Marlowe received this solemn statement with less of gravity than was due to the mysterious nature of the calamity foreshadowed. In truth, he laughed.

"Try to remember," he said. "Maybe you dreamed that Baby had lost the power of speech."

The conjecture was obviously suggested by the fact that Baby, clinging to the fringe of his hunting-coat with all her ten pudgy thumbs, was at that moment uttering her sense of the situation in a series of exultant goo-goos inspired by sight of her father's raccoon-skin cap.

The woman yielded: lacking the gift of humour she could not hold out against his kindly badinage. So, with a kiss for the mother and a kiss for the child, he left the house and closed the door upon his happiness... forever.

At nightfall he had not returned. The woman prepared supper and waited. Then she put Baby to bed and sang softly to her until she slept. By this time the fire on the hearth, at which she had cooked supper, had burned out and the room was lighted by a single candle. This she afterward placed in the open window as a sign and welcome to the hunter if he should approach from that side. She had thoughtfully closed and barred the door against such wild animals as might prefer it to an open window—of the habits of beasts of prey in entering a house uninvited she was not advised, though with true female prevision she may have considered the possibility of their entrance by way of the chimney. As the night wore on she became not less anxious, but more drowsy, and at last rested her arms upon the bed by the child and her head upon the arms. The candle in the window burned down to the socket, sputtered and flared a moment and went out unobserved; for the woman slept and dreamed.

In her dreams she sat beside the cradle of a second child. The first one was dead. The father was dead. The home in the forest was lost and the dwelling in which she lived was unfamiliar. There were heavy oaken doors, always closed, and outside the windows, fastened into the thick stone walls, were iron bars, obviously—so she thought—a provision against intruders. All this she noted with an infinite self-pity, but without surprise—an emotion unknown in dreams. The child in the cradle was invisible under its coverlet which something impelled her to remove. She did so, disclosing the face of a wild animal! In the shock of this dreadful revelation the dreamer awoke, trembling in the darkness of her cabin in the wood.

As a sense of her actual surroundings came slowly back to her, she felt for the child that was not a dream, and assured herself by its breathing that all was well with her; nor could she forbear to pass a hand lightly across her face. Then, moved by some impulse for which she probably could not have accounted, she rose and took the sleeping babe in her arms, holding it close against her breast.

The head of the child's cot was against the wall to which the woman now turned her back as she stood. Lifting her eyes she saw two bright objects starring the darkness with a reddish-green glow. She took them to be two coals on the hearth, but with her returning sense of direction came the disquieting consciousness that they were not in that quarter of the room, moreover were too high, being nearly at the level of the eye of her own eyes. For these were the eyes of a panther.

The beast was at the open window directly opposite and not five paces away. Nothing but those terrible eyes was visible, but in the dreadful tumult of her feelings, as the situation disclosed itself to her understanding, she somehow knew that the animal was standing on its hinder feet, supporting itself with its paws on the window ledge. That signified a malign interest—not the mere gratification of an indolent curiosity. The consciousness of the attitude was an added horror, accentuating the menace of those awful eyes, in whose steadfast fire her strength and courage were alike consumed. Under their silent questioning she shuddered and turned sick. Her knees failed her, and by degrees, instinctively striving to avoid a sudden movement that might bring the beast upon her, she sank to the floor, crouching against the wall to shield the babe with her trembling body without withdrawing her gaze from the luminous orbs. No thought of her husband came to her in her agony—no hope nor suggestion of rescue or escape. Her capacity for thought and feeling had narrowed to the dimensions of a single emotion: fear of the animal's spring, of the impact of its body, the buffeting of its great arms, the feel of its teeth in her throat, the mangling of her babe.

Motionless now and in absolute silence, she awaited her doom, the moments growing to hours, to years, to ages; and still those devilish eyes maintained their watch.

Returning to his cabin late at night with a deer on his shoulders Charles Marlowe tried the door. It did not yield. He knocked; there was no answer. He laid down his deer and went round to the window. As he turned the angle of the building he fancied he heard a sound as of stealthy footfalls and a rustling in thc undcrgrowth of the forest, but they were too slight for certainty, even to his practised ear. Approaching the window, and to his surprise finding it open, he threw his leg over the sill and entered. All was darkness and silence. He groped his way to the fireplace, struck a match and lit a candle.

Then he looked about. Cowering on the floor against a wall was his wife, clasping his daughter.

As he sprang toward her, she rose and broke into laughter, long, loud, and mechanical, devoid of gladness and devoid of sense—the laughter that is not out of keeping with the clanking of a chain. Hardly knowing what he did he extended his arms. She laid the babe in them. She was dead—pressed to death in her mother's embrace.

That is what occurred during a night in a forest, but not all of it did Irene Marlowe relate to Jenner Brading; not all of it was known to her. When she had concluded, the sun was below the horizon and the long summer twilight had begun to deepen in the hollows of the land. For some moments Brading was silent, expecting the narrative to be carried forward to some definite connection with the conversation introducing it; but the narrator was as silent as he, her face averted, her hands clasping and unclasping themselves as they lay in her lap, with a singular suggestion of an activity independent of her will.

"It is a sad, a terrible story," said Brading at last, "but I do not understand. You call Charles Marlowe father; that I know. That he is old before his time, broken by some great sorrow, I have seen, or thought I saw. But, pardon me, you said that you—that you—"

"That I am insane," said the girl, without a movement of head or body.

"But, Irene, you say—please, dear, do not look away from me. You say that the child was dead, not demented."

"Yes, that one—I am the second. I was born three months after that night, my mother being mercifully permitted to lay down her life in giving me mine."

Brading was again silent; he was a trifle dazed and could not at once think of the right thing to say. Her face was still turned away. In his embarrassment he reached impulsively toward the hands that lay closing and unclosing in her lap, but something, he could not have said what, restrained him. He then remembered, vaguely, that he had never altogether cared to take her hand.

"Is it likely," she resumed, "that a person born under such circumstances is like others—is what you call sane?"

Brading did not reply; he was preoccupied with a new thought that was taking shape in his mind—what a scientist would have called an hypothesis; a detective, a theory. It might throw an added light, albeit a lurid one, upon such doubt of her sanity as her own assertion had not dispelled.

The country was still new and, outside the villages, sparsely populated. The professional hunter was still a familiar figure, and among his trophies were heads and pelts of the larger kinds of game. Tales variously credible of nocturnal meetings with savage animals in lonely roads were sometimes current, passed through the customary stages of growth and decay, and were forgotten.

A recent addition to these popular apocrypha, originating, apparently, by spontaneous generation in several households, was of a panther which had frightened some of their members by looking in at windows by night. The yarn had caused its little ripple of excitement—had even attained to the distinction of a place in the local newspaper, but Brading had given it no attention. Its likeness to the story to which he had just listened now impressed him as perhaps more than accidental. Was it not possible that the one story had suggested the other, that finding congenial conditions in a morbid mind and a fertile fancy, it had grown to the tragic tale that he had heard?

Brading recalled certain circumstances of the girl's history and disposition, of which, with love's incuriosity, he had hitherto been heedless—such as her solitary life with her father, at whose house no one, apparently, was an acceptable visitor and her strange fear of the night, by which those who knew her best accounted for her never being seen after dark.

Surely in such a mind, imagination once kindled might burn with a lawless flame, penetrating and enveloping the entire structure. That she was mad, though the conviction gave him the acutest pain, he could no longer doubt; she had only mistaken an effect of her mental disorder for its cause, bringing into imaginary relation with her own personality the vagaries of the local mythmakers. With some vague intention of testing his new "theory," and no very definite notion of how to set about it, he said, gravely, but with hesitation:

"Irene, dear, tell me. I beg you will not take offence, but tell me—"

"I have told you," she interrupted, speaking with a passionate earnestness that he had not known her to show. "I have already told you that we cannot marry; is anything else worth saying?"

Before he could stop her she had sprung from her seat and without another word or look was gliding away among the trees toward her father's house. Brading had risen to detain her; he stood watching her in silence until she had vanished in the gloom. Suddenly he started as if he had been shot. His face took on an expression of amazement and alarm. In one of the black shadows into which she had disappeared he had caught a quick, brief glimpse of shining eyes! For an instant he was dazed and irresolute; then he dashed into the wood after her, shouting: "Irene, Irene, look out! The panther! The panther!"

In a moment he had passed through the fringe of forest into open ground and saw the girl's gray skirt vanishing into her father's door. No panther was visible.

Jenner Brading, attorney-at-law, lived in a cottage at the edge of the town. Directly behind the dwelling was the forest. Being a bachelor, and therefore, by the Draconian moral code of the time and place, denied the services of the only species of domestic servant known thereabout, the "hired girl," he boarded at the village hotel, where also was his office. The woodside cottage was merely a lodging maintained at no great cost, to be sure as an evidence of prosperity and respectability.

It would hardly do for one to whom the local newspaper had pointed with pride as "the foremost jurist of his time" to be "homeless," albeit he may sometimes have suspected that the words "home" and "house" were not strictly synonymous. Indeed, his consciousness of the disparity and his will to harmonize it were matters of logical inference, for it was generally reported that soon after the cottage was built, its owner had made a futile venture in the direction of marriage—had, in truth, gone so far as to be rejected by the beautiful but eccentric daughter of Old Man Marlowe, the recluse. This was publicly believed because he had told it himself and she had not—a reversal of the usual order of things which could hardly fail to carry conviction.

Brading's bedroom was at the rear of the house, with a single window facing the forest.

One night he was awakened by a noise at that window; he could hardly have said what it was like. With a little thrill of the nerves he sat up in bed and laid hold of the revolver which, with a forethought most commendable in one addicted to the habit of sleeping on the ground floor with an open window, he had put under his pillow. The room was in absolute darkness, but being un-terrified he knew where to direct his eyes, and there he held them, awaiting in silence what further might occur.

He could now dimly discern a form—a square of lighter black. Presently there appeared at its lower edge two gleaming eyes that burned with a malignant lustre, inexpressibly terrible! Brading's heart gave a great jump, then seemed to stand still. A chill passed along his spine and through his hair; he felt the blood forsake his cheeks. He could not have cried out—not to save his life; but being a man of courage he would not, to save his life, have done so if he had been able. Some trepidation his coward body might feel, but his spirit was of sterner stuff. Slowly the shining eyes rose with a steady motion that seemed an approach, and slowly rose Brading's right hand, holding the pistol. He fired!

Blinded by the flash and stunned by the report, Brading nevertheless heard, or fancied that he heard, the wild, high scream of the panther, so human in sound, so devilish in suggestion. Leaping from the bed he hastily clothed himself and, pistol in hand, sprang from the door, meeting two or three men who came running up from the road. A brief explanation was followed by a cautious search of the house. The grass was wet with dew; beneath the window, it had been trodden and partly leveled for a wide space, from which a devious trail, visible in the light of a lantern, led away into the bushes. One of the men stumbled and fell upon his hands, which, as he rose and rubbed them together, were slippery. On examination they were seen to be red with blood.

An encounter, unarmed, with a wounded panther was not agreeable to their taste; all but Brading turned back. He, with lantern and pistol, pushed courageously forward into the wood. Passing through a difficult undergrowth he came into a small opening, and there his courage had its reward, for there he found the body of his victim. But it was no panther.

What it was is told, even to this day, upon a weather-worn headstone in the village churchyard, and for many years was attested daily at the graveside by the bent figure and sorrow-seamed face of Old Man Marlowe, to whose soul, and to the soul of his strange, unhappy child, peace. Peace and reparation.

ABOUT THE AUTHORS

Also about the musicians and performers of the Audiobook edition of Secrets of the Forsaken. Durvile.com provides audiobook links and samples.

PART ONE. Secrets Unearthed: Original Writings

Chapter 1. "The Knock of Damnation"
Author, Narrator, Music: Julian Hobson. Julian was born in Sheffield, UK. He now lives off-grid along the slopes of the Rockies, sharing his time between his profession as a cardiac sonographer, his practice of hypnotherapy, and nature. Julian co-edited the book, *Embrace Your Divine Flow: Evolvements for Healing.*

Chapter 2. "The Beach"
Author, Narrator, Soundscape: Lorene Shyba. Lorene is publisher at Durvile & UpRoute, a culmination of a career that includes being an international theatre impresario, video producer, magazine art director, TV talent, parent, digital art curator, and university professor. She co-edited *Indigenous Justice* and *Ascenti: Humans Opening to AI.*

Chapter 3. "Rising Wolf"
Author, Narrator, Soundscape: Jared Tailfeathers. Jared is a distinguished Blackfoot multidisciplinary artist whose creative pursuits include art, music, literature, curation, and invention. He is the author of *The Art of Making* and his art and music website can be found at tailfeathersart.com

Chapter 4. "Dead Hed"
Author, Narrator: Cary Thomas Cody. Cary Thomas Cody is a writer, director, storyteller, and filmmaker from the Kiowa Tribe of Oklahoma. His goal is to tell stories through short films, podcasts, around the campfire, and on the page in *Whistle at Night and They Will Come.* Find Cary's work at youtube.com/@theskullcrawlers.

Chapter 5. "The Táltos"
Author, Narrator: Jessica Theroux. Music: Kenna Burima. Jessica is an artist and educator acclaimed for her ability to blend personal joys and freedoms with her creative endeavours. She is the author and artist behind the book *Goddess Alpha: Directions Home.* Kenna Burima is a writer, teacher, and musician. Her album "While She Sleeps" is available on Spotify. She also wrote a chapter about music and AI for the book *Ascenti: Humans Opening to AI.*

Chapter 6. "The Wisdom of Nahganne"
Author: Raymond Yakeleya. Narrator: John Heerema. Raymond Yakeleya is from the Sahtu Dene Nation of Northwest Territories. His books include *The Tree by the Woodpile, We Remember the Coming of the White Man, The Rainbow, the Midwife and the Birds,* and *Indigenous Justice.* John Heerema is a narration performer, photographer and software developer. He wrote a story about photography and AI for the book *Ascenti: Humans Opening to AI.*

Chapter 7. "The Theatre of Sacrifice"
Author, Performer: Maeve Wills. Maeve has a background in theatre, with a concentration on performance and multimedia. She is also an audio editor and engineer with Pepper Ranch Studios, along with her brother Marcus.

Chapter 8. "Rising Sun"
Author: Alex Soop. Performed by Cary Thomas Cody. Alex Soop of the Blackfoot Confederacy voices his stories from First Nations Peoples' perspective. While striving to entertain with his bloodcurdling tales, he also integrates issues that plague Indigenous Peoples. He is the author of *Midnight Storm Moonless Sky* and *Whistle at Night and They Will Come*.

Chapter 9. "Threads in the Shadows"
Author and Narrator: Laurier Tiernan. Interdisciplinary artist Laurier Tiernan divides his time between Tokyo, Japan, and Edmonton, Alberta. He is the author of the bilingual graphic poetry book *Fifty-Five Ways to Survive | Cinquante-cinq voies de survie*. His music can be heard on his Youtube channel at youtube.com/c/TiernanSongs

Chapter 10. "Tough Love"
Author: Lynda Partridge. Narrator: Lorene Shyba. Lynda is a member of the Algonquins of Pikwakanagan First Nation. Lynda's kids' books are *Lillian & Kokomis; Why Are You Still Here; and Spirit Rider*. Her story for *Secrets of the Forsaken* also appeared in *Embrace Your Divine Flow*. Her website is lyndapartridge.ca.

Chapter 11. "The Trainride"
Author: Uchechukwu Umezurike. Narrator: Julian Hobson. Uche is an assistant professor in the Department of English at the University of Calgary. He is the 2021 winner of the Nigeria Prize for Literary Criticism. His story for *Secrets of the Forsaken* also appeared in the book *Ascenti: Humans Opening to AI.*

Chapter 12. "Twisted into a Scapegoat"
Author: John L. Hill. Narrator: John Heerema. John Hill is a retired Canadian lawyer renowned for his work in criminal and prison law, representing penitentiary inmates and handling Canada's most complex cases. Throughout his career, Hill tackled high-profile issues like solitary confinement and wrongful convictions. He is the author of *Pine Box Parole* and *Acts of Darkness.*

Chapter 13. "A Martyr's Reckoning"
Author: James R. Parker. Narrator: Austin Andrews. Jim is a professor of art at the University of Calgary whose expertise ranges from computer simulation, AI, and generative art. He is author of *Generative Art Algorithms, Generative Art: Python,* and contributor in *RumbleSat, Embrace Your Divine Flow,* and *Ascenti.* Austin Andrews is a film director and editor. His website is flickertheory.com.

PART TWO. Echoes of the Departed: Timeless Tales

Chapter 14. "Paranormal Encounters: Uncharted North"
Authors: Samuel de Champlain et al. Narrated by Lorene Shyba, Julian Hobson, and Marcus Wills. Explorers' journal entries are by Samuel de Champlain (1609 and 1613), Henry Hudson (1608 and1611), David Thompson (1811), Lewis and Clark (1804 and 1805), Sir John Franklin (1821 and 1845), and Alexander Mackenzie (1793).

Chapter 15. "The Horror of Frankenstein"
Author: Mary Shelley. Narrator: Lorene Shyba. Mary Shelley was an English author best known for her groundbreaking novel *Frankenstein* (1818), which explored themes of scientific ambition, creation, and moral responsibility. Shelley was a pioneering figure in Gothic literature and an influential voice in early science fiction

Chapter 16. "A Haunted House"
Author: Virginia Woolf. Narrator: Lorene Shyba. Virginia Woolf was a British author whose works revolutionized narrative techniques with her use of stream of consciousness. A key figure in the Bloomsbury Group, Woolf explored themes of identity, time, and the human psyche in her fiction and essays. She wrote the short story "A Haunted House" in 1921.

Chapter17. "In a Grove"
Author: Ryūnosuke Akutagawa. Narrator: Laurier Tiernan. Ryūnosuke Akutagawa was a Japanese author known as the father of the Japanese short story, whose works, often rooted in historical themes, explored human nature, morality, and perception. He wrote "In a Grove" (*Yabu no Naka*) in 1921.

Chapter 18. "A Vision of Horror"
Author: Helena Blavatsky. Narrator: Lorene Shyba. Helena Blavatsky was a mystic, philosopher, and co-founder of the Theosophical Society. Her writings combined esoteric philosophy, spirituality, and the occult. She sought to bridge Eastern and Western spiritual traditions. She wrote "A Vision of Horror" in 1878.

Chapter 19. "A Ghost Story"
Author: Mark Twain. Narrator: Marcus Wills. Mark Twain (1835–1910), born Samuel Langhorne Clemens, was an iconic American author and humourist best known for *The Adventures of Tom Sawyer* and *Adventures of Huckleberry Finn.* He wrote the short story "A Ghost Story" in 1870.

Chapter 20. "The Eyes of the Panther"
Author: Ambrose Bierce. Narrator: Maeve Wills. Ambrose Bierce was an American author, journalist, and satirist renowned for his darkly imaginative short stories, particularly those with themes of horror and the supernatural. He wrote "The Eyes of the Panther" in 1897 and it was first published in his collection *Can Such Things Be?*

Chapter 21. "The Signal-Man" *(Bonus audiobook and website feature)* Author: Charles Dickens. Narrator: Julian Hobson. Charles Dickens was a celebrated English novelist and social critic who vividly portrayed Victorian society and explored themes of class, morality, and human resilience. He wrote "The Signal-Man" in 1866.

BIBLIOGRAPHY

Original Stories

Partridge, Lynda. “Tough Love,” *Embrace Your Divine Flow,* 183–194. Calgary: Durvile, 2023.

Soop, Alex. “Rising Sun,” *Whistle at Night and They Will Come,* 25–36. Calgary: Durvile, 2023.

Uchechukwu Peter Umezurike, “A Trainride is a Lifetime,” *Ascenti: Humans Opening to AI,* 44–57. Calgary: Durvile, 2024.

Classic Stories

Akutagawa, Ryūnosuke. “In a Grove.” Tokyo: *Shincho,* January 1922.

Bierce, Ambrose. “The Eyes of the Panther.” *Can Such Things Be?* New York: Harper & Brothers, 1893.

Champlain, Samuel de. *Les Voyages de la Nouvelle France Occidentale, dite Canada.* Paris: Claude Collet, 1632.

Franklin, John. *Narrative of a Journey to the Shores of the Polar Sea in the Years 1819, 20, 21, and 22.* London: John Murray, 1823.

Hudson, Henry. "Journal of Henry Hudson's 1608 Voyage." In *Purchas His Pilgrimes, vol.* 3. London: William Stansby for Henrie Fetherstone, 1625.

Lewis, Meriwether, and William Clark. *The Journals of the Lewis and Clark Expedition, 1804-1806.* Originally archived in manuscript form; selections first published in *History of the Expedition Under the Command of Captains Lewis and Clark,* Philadelphia: Bradford and Inskeep, 1814.

Mackenzie, Alexander. *Voyages from Montreal... to the Frozen and Pacific Oceans in 1789 and 1793.* London: T. Cadell Jr. and W. Davies, 1801.

Shelley, Mary. *Frankenstein; or, The Modern Prometheus.* London: Lackington, Hughes, Harding, Mavor & Jones, 1818.

Thompson, David. *Narrative of His Explorations in Western America 1784-1812.* Manuscript completed c. 1847; first published by Champlain Society, Toronto, 1916.

Twain, Mark. "A Ghost Story." *Sketches New and Old,* 289-296. Hartford, CT: American Publishing Company, 1875.
Woolf, Virginia. "A Haunted House." *Monday or Tuesday.* London: Hogarth Press, 1921.

Durvile & UpRoute: "Every River Lit" series

"Ways of Light and Darkness" titles

Ways

of

Light and

Darkness

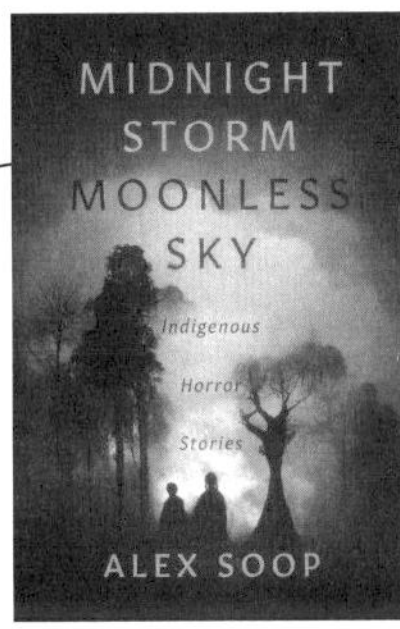

DURVILE & UpRoute
"bright" books with bite

DURVILE.COM